The Battle of Zig Zag Pass

SPEAKING VOLUMES, LLC
NAPLES, FLORIDA
2021

The Battle of Zig Zag Pass

Cover design by Hannah Linder

ISBN 978-1-64540-564-1

The Battle of Zig Zag Pass

C. H. Boyer

This book is dedicated to Prof. Margaret Ann Pursell

Chapter One

What do you think, Sergeant?

Same old shit, sir. Fire and maneuver. You take those guys up on the left side. I'll take these guys up on the right. Fire and maneuver.

What if the 'fire and maneuver' drill breaks down?

It always does. We just keep pounding away till whatever they're doing breaks down, too.

***

I instinctively fear my first day of anything, and war is right up there. So, I couldn't tell the young Sergeant what I was really thinking. I wanted to be somewhere else at that moment, somewhere safe, writing a comedy and sipping a cold drink. I had started out writing comedies; well, stealing cars and then writing comedies. But the war started, and then I was an Army Captain getting ready to lead a small part of what later became The Battle of Zig Zag Pass.

The word "small" here should not be overlooked. The main battle was way the hell over there somewhere, on the Philippine mainland. That's where most of the Japs were and where most of our guys were. That's also where the ziggy zaggy mountain road was that gave this venture its short mention in the history of WWII.

No one today knows anything about The Battle of Zig Zag Pass, and no one even back then knew much about the five or six little side actions taking place on a half-dozen surrounding islands, more or less in support of the bigger battle.

My job was to take a reinforced company of infantry, about 200 guys, and go with the Navy aboard a small transport, called an LCI, for

Landing Craft Infantry, and knock out a Jap artillery battery. This so-called battery could have dropped some shells on our guys over on the mainland, so it needed to be dealt with ASAP.

As we approached shallow water and waited for the bow doors to open so we could storm the beach, we didn't know that there wasn't any battery there. What was there was just a light Jap tank with its little 37mm gun. It would have been nice to know this ahead of time, because I didn't have the reinforced company of hard-boiled infantry that I was supposed to have.

No one in war ever gets what they want.

General Clausewitz called that friction, and the old guy knew what he was talking about. What I got was just ten soldiers and two clerks we grabbed along the way to beef up our attack. In the Army, no matter what your job is, you are supposed to remember how to be a badass infantry soldier. That's not true, of course, as human nature doesn't play like that. But I had just lectured the two clerks, and told them that it was so, and they seemed to buy it.

Fortunately for us, that Jap tank had already been struck by one of our artillery rounds fired from the mainland, and the tank commander and his gunner were slowly bleeding to death. The rest of the tank crew and a few supporting Jap infantry had scattered deeper into the jungle, which meant they weren't far away. You could throw a baseball across this island if you had a good arm and someone cut all the trees down.

We didn't know any of this as the LCI pulled right up to the beach. The big doors swung out left and right and we started to run down a small ramp and through about two feet of beach water. That's about all I would ever recall of the entire day.

As we started up the beach, the Navy guys on the foredeck twenty feet above us began banging away with their 20mm anti-aircraft guns, shooting some pretty big lead right over our heads and into the green on the other side of the narrow beach. They were really unloading on whoever might be hiding in there, and we were more than glad to have the help.

I'm sure they also wanted to protect their ship, which was as vulnerable as a bathtub sitting there in the sand.

This was a minuscule operation, but one of the givens about war is that even one bullet coming in your general direction makes it a big war.

As I scrambled up the beach slope, one of those 20mm rounds hit the frame of a Jap truck that had been abandoned just inside the tree line. A hot chunk of something caromed off at an angle and hit me in the lower back just as I turned around to the ship to tell them to lift their fire. That was the beginning and end of The Battle of Zig Zag Pass for me, and the beginning and end of my war. Except for the fact that I would be paralyzed in the legs for the rest of my life, I thought, looking back on it sometime later, that this wasn't a comedy, but it was funny.

In a war kind of way.

Chapter Two

Do you know who I am?

You're the Dean of Students.

That's excellent. You would be surprised how many of our students cannot answer that question correctly. And do you know what I do here?

You expel students.

You must be a prodigy. Yes, that's all the Dean of Students does. Not many know that. From morning till 5 in the afternoon, till 7 on Thursdays, I sit here and expel students. Do you know why you're sitting here?

Was it something I did?

Oh, my goodness. Why do the best and brightest end up in my office?

***

The Battle of Zig Zag Pass began and ended in the Philippines in 1945. It was between us and the Japs. We won.

My part in The Battle of Zig Zag Pass began earlier, in 1932, in a small liberal arts college in Michigan, called Albion, one of the old names for good old England.

My name is Lloyd Zadoc. Call me Lord. I'll explain the Lord thing later. I was a TEKE at Albion. That's for TKE, Tau Kappa Epsilon, the best fraternity on campus. We were the elite of our day.

My job at the fraternity that semester—I was a junior—was to put our new pledges through a ritual hazing.

These pledges were sophomores, good men, chosen to maintain the special quality of our TKE house. I had twelve of them on the back deck of the house at two o'clock in the morning, in their underwear, on their knees and blindfolded. Each pledge was given a pitcher of warm beer and told to chug it.

This alone isn't the worst thing you can do to a pledge. But our back deck made it more interesting. Part of it overlooks a straight 16-foot drop to a brick-paved parking lot. Another part of it overlooks a six-inch drop to a grassy walkway. We, of course, told them they were teetering over the parking lot, and anyone who lost his balance and fell forward would either die or spend the rest of his life in a wheelchair. Anyone who fell backward toward safety would be blackballed on the spot, and never become a TKE.

Before we handed out all the beer, a kid named Punky Harrison, a budding genius in physics, fell forward, letting out a terrible yell, and landed six inches below on the grass. We laughed until we realized that Punky had gone into some kind of catatonic shock. We finally had to haul him off to the infirmary, where they declared he was paralyzed from the waist down.

That wasn't the worst part. While Punky was screaming and making awful noises, the other pledges took off their blind folds to watch. That's when the pledge leader, a pre-law student named Don Bayer, made his offhand remark—the words that got me thrown out of Albion. Looking over the scene, still on his knees, Bayer looked at me and said, "Why is it always the weakest cowards who seem to enjoy this the most?"

I walked over to him, placed my foot squarely in his back and sent him—a rich kid from Detroit—flying over the six-inch drop.

Our fraternity president, Randolph Levy, a goody-two-shoes from the Upper Peninsula, saw me, and instead of dealing with it in-house, he reported me to the Dean of Students.

I think he did that to drop the blame for Punky's paralysis on me. The son of a bitch. After I got expelled, Punky got out of bed and started walking. The son of a bitch.

Chapter Three

So, you're a college kid.

I was *a college kid. I got thrown out for paralyzing a guy.*

Ooh, tough guy. What makes you think you're as tough as we are? With you college boys, it's all a game. Out here, you're either tough or you're dead.

Try me.

Okay. Go steal a car that looks like something you can't afford to be driving.

***

My first trial was so easy anyone could have done it. And I had to do it. It was now 1933. The entire economy had gone down the drain. A lot of the banks had closed, cutting off savings and deposits people would never see again. Families and businesses were wiped out overnight, just like that.

I had been thrown out of college and didn't have a job. I signed on with this gang of rum runners. My job was to help them get booze across the bridge from Windsor, Ontario to Detroit. It was still the Prohibition Era in the States, though it would finally end later that year. Meanwhile, there was some serious money to be made.

My job was to drive in from Canada in an expensive car in the middle of the night. The U.S. Customs guys would likely swarm all over me. A couple minutes behind me, in an old Ford, a fake mother and dad and some sleeping kids would drive up. While the customs guys were trying to take my car apart, they'd wave the old Ford on through to Detroit. The Ford had all the booze inside it.

But where was I going to steal an expensive car? I only knew one really rich kid, Bayer, back at Albion. He had a bright yellow Packard De Luxe Super 8 Seven Passenger sedan, an ostentatious mobster car with pull-down privacy shades and big spare wheels mounted in streamlined shells on each running board. Piece of cake. I caught a lift back to Albion, tiptoed into the old TKE house at two a.m. and tiptoed out with the keys to my new Packard.

I didn't feel bad. Bayer owed me.

Over the next three months, I made a dozen midnight crossings from Canada and the deal came off like a charm. Each time, the agents surrounded me, and they let the old Ford with the family full of sleeping kids go right on through—with the booze.

The next time around, though, the customs guys started to wake up. They just glanced at my papers and waved me through. In my rearview mirror, I saw them signal the Ford to pull over for an inspection.

Shit.

When I got to the warehouse on Nine Mile Road in Detroit a half hour later, I told the gang what happened. Instead of panicking, they just laughed. Two of them walked over and pulled out the Packard's backseat. Tucked under there were about six dozen bottles of booze.

What the hell?

"You fooled 'em good tonight, college boy."

The sons of bitches. I quit the gang right then and there. But I kept Bayer's Packard.

Chapter Four

Do you know who I am?

Yeah, you're a cop.

You see all these little stars on my collar? I'm the chief of police of the whole city of Detroit. I'm the big dog. Do you know why a little guy like you is sitting in front of a big dog like me?

I jacked a boiler. Big deal.

You didn't just steal a car, son, you stole a '31 Packard De Luxe 8, and you used it to hustle booze from Canada.

Is that such a crime?

You're about to find out, wise guy. I want the name and location of your colleagues.

They didn't tell me their names, and I forgot where they go to church.

Well, don't worry about it too much. We're going to send you to a nice quiet place where you can relax and refresh your memory.

***

My mistake was stopping for a damn candy bar. I was slow cruising through downtown Detroit, trying to figure out how to sell the Packard without the usual polite paperwork. So many factories and businesses had closed by then, so the city was full of people out of work.

I saw a guy at the curb with a sign selling Chicken Dinner candy bars. I always liked Chicken Dinner candy bars. I pulled over and motioned for him to come closer.

The sidewalk was awash in stony-faced people trying to sell everything from apples to rags and candy bars. The Depression was getting worse, and people were scared.

The candy bar guy had on a leather jacket, and before he leaned down where I could see his face, I saw the TKE pin. A TKE! And then there he was—knit tie, combed air, intelligent, handsome face—Bayer.

"Bayer, what the hell are you doing selling candy bars?"

"What are you doing driving my car, Zadoc?"

I suddenly lost my sense of perspective, jumped out of the car and began yelling at him, toe to toe. I told him he was a disgrace and an embarrassment to the TKE house. Bayer, to give him credit, kept his sense of perspective intact and called to a policeman on the opposite corner.

During the couple minutes before the cops sent a car to get me, Bayer told me his dad had lost everything in the market crash and bank closures. The works. Overnight, rich Don Bayer went from a tennis-playing junior at Albion to just another sad sack, selling Chicken Dinner candy bars on the street.

And I went upstate for a few years. It was my first time inside a real prison, but it wasn't my first time upstate. I'd been there before, as a kid. I never did get my Chicken Dinner candy bar, and it rankled me for days.

Chapter Five

Remember Lord Zadoc, we are all God's children.
I don't think I'm one of God's children.
And why not?
I'm an orphan.

***

Everyone who knows me calls me Lord. That's because a childhood friend, an elementary school buddy, called me Lord. To this day, I don't know what his problem was. He either couldn't hear well, wasn't good with languages, or was a tad soft in the head.

I didn't like being called Lord. And I suppose because I didn't like it, it caught on and spread as I went through school, until it just become part of me. I tried, but I couldn't figure out how to duck away from it and resurface somewhere else as plain old, but distinguished, Lloyd.

Back in my tender years, I believed, without knowing why, that the name Lloyd had a noble aura—long before I knew what "noble aura" meant. Anyhow, it made my young ego angry to be called Lord. It riled me enough to drag fat-assed Derrick, for that was the name of the blinker, out to the front lawn of my aunt's house. That's where I threw a pretty well executed hangman's noose around his neck—I had practiced for weeks making that noose—and threw the other end of the rope up and over a large shady branch of her red maple tree. Then, I started pulling hard on the rope, trying to hang him.

Even through the solid walls of her house, my aunt, a Christian woman with a hefty German build, sensed the danger. She came running out the front door in her apron and pulled the rope out of my hands with one hand and delivered an amazing wallop to my face with the other. Just like that. My fate as "Lord" was sealed.

Shortly after that, I ended up in one of those schools you have to live in until you are 18 years old. The school master went to great lengths to explain that it wasn't a "reform school," but I knew it was a reform school. I don't want to talk about those years.

Let me just say that Babe Ruth had a better time of it in his Catholic orphanage than I did at the Upper Peninsula School for Boys. The only thing Ruth had worse was that he went to the orphanage from a home where both of his parents lived with his siblings. That always struck me as cruel.

I only had my aunt. My parents and my three sisters died the night our family house burned down, but I don't want to talk about that.

To be fair to my aunt, she didn't enroll me in UP for Boys. The state had me "committed" to the place, primarily because I tried to string up Derrick the malaprop. There were more reasons than that, according to the state guy.

My aunt was actually a pretty nice lady. It's just that all those other things—okay, they were stolen cars—started to pile up on her and cause her some grief. So, I can't blame her for doing what she did.

I stashed the money I made from the stolen cars in mason jars buried in the ground. That's how I paid for Albion, later on. There was a little more to it than that, but I don't want to talk about it.

Chapter Six

You're lucky, Zadoc.

Why is that?

You're not only getting out early because of the war; you're going to Infantry Officer Candidate School because you were a college man.

You call that lucky?

What's the worst that could happen?

***

Prison had been pretty much like reform school, except you didn't have to listen to everyone cry themselves to sleep at night. Still, I was glad to get out of there. Prisons are noisy, they never turn off the lights, and the temperature is either too hot or too cold. And you're never quite sure about the neighbors.

Freedom had a price, though. I had to enlist. Big deal. Everyone was enlisting in 1942. It felt like the right thing to do. It even felt kind of good. I just hoped I would be sent to Europe and not the Pacific. The Japs were crazy. No one wanted to deal with lunatics.

Unlike most officer candidates for the infantry, I liked to read. My fellow students, mostly young sergeants and corporals who had shown some promise, simply wanted to earn their officer commissions to avoid living—and often dying—at the low end of the military pole. Just after I arrived at Fort Benning, Georgia, I went to the base library and stole their copy of Clausewitz's *On War*, a 900-page door stopper. In it, I found the answer to every miserable situation that could befall an infantry officer.

While my fellow officer candidate students were memorizing the small stuff—how to organize a patrol, how to keep track of distance, how to navigate with a compass, and so on, I concentrated on how to defend a mountain, how to attack a mountain, how to defend a river, how to attack a river. I sought the big picture, the key to the puzzle of war; how to concentrate my forces at the vital spot at the right moment.

I read late into the night. *On War*, is not only 900 pages; it's written in that awful, overstuffed parlor language from way back in the 1800s.

"The influence of mountains on the conduct of war is very great: the subject, therefore, is very important for theory. As this influence introduces into action a retarding principle, it belongs chiefly to the defensive. We shall therefore discuss it here in a wider sense than that conveyed by the simple conception, defense of mountains. As we have discovered in our consideration of the subject results which run counter to general opinion in many points, we shall therefore be obliged to enter into rather an elaborate analysis of it."

See what I mean? It's no wonder I fell sound asleep in Officer's class one sultry Georgia afternoon. The officer-candidate next to me grabbed my arm and shook it hard, whispering, "The instructor just called your name. The answer is 'mortars and heavy machine guns, followed by small arms firing at targets at will.' "

I jumped to my feet.

"Sir, mortars and heavy machine guns, followed by small arms firing at targets at will."

I could tell in a microsecond, from the look on the Major's face, that he had not called on anyone, and I had just made a fool of myself by interrupting his lecture. Fortunately, the Major had been around the block and returned as a good guy.

"That's not a bad answer, Zadoc. You hang onto it, and I'm sure you'll find it will come in handy someday at the right time under the right circumstances."

For a brief second, just before I sat down, I thought about quoting something from Clausewitz, but then thought, *the hell with it.*

I graduated third in my class, got commissioned as a Second Lieutenant of Infantry, and received orders to join a division on its way to fight the Japs in the Pacific.

Before I left, I took the copy of Clausewitz back to the library.

Chapter Seven

You've got a severe spinal cord injury at the T-12 vertebrae, a thoracic injury.

How do you know?

I took a big chunk of metal out of there a couple days ago. You may be paralyzed from the waist down.

Are you a surgeon?

No, I'm the corpsman on this ship. But I did three years of medical school before the war.

Will I be able to get an erection?

Yes, possibly, but . . .

But what?

You probably won't be able to do much with it.

***

Other than lying face down and trying to pee into a folded towel, I wasn't particularly annoyed with my new situation. With all the time I'd spent in institutions (a word I'd like take out of circulation) I was somewhat used to having my ass hanging out in semipublic places.

But hey, I was alive. I had a legitimate injury—not some Halloween Party charade. Couple of months on crutches, maybe an operation, some rehabilitation. I survived the war with a purple heart.

Could have been worse.

Then it got worse.

Heinz Arborgast, the 24-year-old corpsman, told me I wouldn't be transferred to a Navy hospital ship because I couldn't be moved for a few more days *and* there weren't any hospital ships around. Everything afloat was either at a place called Iwo Jima, and everything that wasn't there was getting ready for another invasion, which turned out to be Okinawa.

At least the other twelve soldiers in our little assault got out okay. They had been picked up by a sister LCI while I was under sedation. They came through the two-hour firefight unscathed but for one missing finger—the Sergeant's—a twisted ankle and a broken jawbone.

A soldier, thinking he saw a sniper, hit the ground fast and landed face first on a rock-hard eucalyptus stump. The sniper turned out to be one of two Japs who tried to surrender. The others committed suicide or died from their wounds. The two surrendering Japs were shot dead where they stood. Our guys were still trying to even the score for countless stories about Japs cutting off the heads and hands of American prisoners.

Some of the stories were a lot worse than that.

"So, what happens now, Heinz?" The kid struck me as unusually competent, but that could have been the wishful thinking of a prone patient.

("They say my doctor is the best in the world.")

"I'm not sure, Sir. We can get the wound patched up so you can at least turn over. That is if . . ."

"What?"

"If it doesn't get infected. But the good news is, that piece of metal was red hot when it went in. Which was good. It cauterized the area. At least it appeared to. I'll know in a day or so. This is kind of fourth-year-course stuff, and I had to leave after three years."

"What course is that?"

"Pulling crap out of people's asses."

"Of course."

"After I see some healing, we'll figure out what works and what doesn't. Hopefully, we'll get you transferred to a hospital ship by then."

"When can I roll over, Heinz?"

"Be patient. You've been really good so far. Tonight, you can have a couple bites of real food. See if we can get your ass back in the ballgame, so to speak, Sir."

The LCI had taken a glancing round on its bow doors, fired by the dying crew on the Jap tank. In the two days it took to make repairs, the ship had settled deeper into the sand, helped by four cycles of rising and falling tides. Now, the combination of shallow water and sand held the hull in a powerful suction. I could hear the crew working all day and through the night, digging and using water hoses to try to break it loose.

Heinz told me that as soon as we could get under way, the captain was going to try to find a way to get me to a hospital on the Philippine mainland. But he hadn't found one yet.

"Captain Bayer checked on local hospitals in Manila," Heinz said, "but the Japs burned them and killed a lot of the staff. We don't know where the Army has set up their field units because we don't use the same radio frequencies."

"Captain who?"

"The skipper, Lieutenant Bayer."

Chapter Eight

What's the captain's first name?
I think it's Don.
Don Bayer the TKE?
I think he's a Christian.

***

This is a small predicament the great Clausewitz overlooked in his epic work.

"Old wars folding into new wars, but on a personal level."

Could it really be that Bayer was the skipper of this ship? What were the odds?

I wanted to dwell on this news, but it felt like getting hit in the back all over again. I did the only thing I could do in that moment. I went back to sleep. For two days and nights now, since regaining consciousness, I had listened to and felt the work and rhythms of the ship.

Stuck in the shallow surf, the bow held in an airtight clamp of wet sand, the LCI echoed every voice, every movement, every metallic thunk. The top deck crews and the men from the engine room worked on either side of the ship, trying to break it free. There seemed to be a natural competition between the two groups. The engine room boys seemed more logical and technical. I heard them talking about pressure points, center of gravity, and gallons per minute. The kids working the other side of the ship—and to me their prattle sounded like kids—tackled their chore as a game.

"Come on Burnzy. Turn up the water pressure. They're making us look bad over there."

Lower, quieter tones seemed to indicate the officers. I heard some talk about shifting fuel from one tank to another, or flooding a tank, something like that. An Ensign called Hennessey, who seemed to go by "Hen" among the other officers, sounded like he was everywhere on the ship. Another, Watkins, appeared to be at loose ends. His voice came up infrequently and no one seemed to engage him when he did talk. Several times I heard a deeper, quieter voice, accompanied by the smell of pipe smoke. Could that be Lt. Bayer? I couldn't be sure.

Heinz told me the main problem was the nature of the sand. It was very fine, almost clay-like. The primary method of pulling the ship off the beach involved dropping a stern anchor several yards out as they approached the beach. Winching in this anchor was supposed to help them break away from their landing. But the stern anchor wasn't grabbing the sea bottom.

I was still a bit feverish and woozy, but I remember hearing myself say, "There are bits of an old rock pier about 50 yards astern and twenty or so yards to the right. Try anchoring on that."

When I awoke again, still lying on my stomach, everything had changed. The pulses of aniline odors from the beach, the burned-out tank, and the dead Japs, were gone. The sticky heat was gone, too. Warm but refreshing air flowed around the cabin. I still noticed the oily diesel fuel smell that permeated everything—even the steel bulkheads—but now it was mixed with patches of fresh saltwater air.

I could feel the engines down below, vibrating, just slightly out of synch. Sailors were moving about the ship, which now swayed pleasantly. I distinctly heard Mr. Hennessey giving orders, his voice rising and falling from below deck. Best of all, I smelled coffee. Then I heard an officer ask Mr. Watkins if they were lost yet—and laugh at his own jest. He told him he could still see land so the ship can't be too far off course. I didn't hear Watkins' reply.

I heard a lot more than this. From years of languishing in institutions, I had taught myself to listen for the dominant nature of things—who was calling the shots, and who was getting shot. From the pace of footsteps and the short, matter of fact voices, the economy of movement, and the level of human energy, you could easily tell this crew had been at it for a long time. They knew what they were doing, and they seemed to have worked out the easiest and best way to do things. There was a fluid, practiced choreography to their actions.

From the way the sailors spoke with the officers, you could tell the ranks anticipated what had to be done. They didn't have to be led. Duty seemed to emanate from a sense of expectation—a level of morale and discipline I'd seen in the infantry only once, among Marines. These men had been working and living together at war for more than two years. Their restricted movements aboard a ship no more than 160 feet long had carved out well-worn patterns of communal life—dining, washing, standing watch, tending the engines, chipping paint, organizing supplies, radio messages, oiling the 20mm guns . . .

To me it felt like a long-running play and all the actors knew their lines and their roles, save one, an officer named Watkins. I got the feeling he was the ship's designated screw-up.

I also got a little bit of a read on the captain, Navy Lieutenant Bayer. By his voice, I could tell he was older than the other officers. But I couldn't tell if this Bayer was my Bayer from Detroit. The odds seemed too long. My imagination, however, wouldn't abide the laws of probability. It was Bayer. I knew it was. And here I was, face down and paralyzed on his ship. You can't make this stuff up.

The officers who occupied quarters next to me joked and laughed a lot, but not like fraternity brothers. They were more subdued, more serious, even when they laughed. They had the Japs to worry about, of course, and in three dimensions: subs, ships, and planes.

They knew they weren't anyone's prize target. But they had another enemy right in front of them—the sea itself.

I heard one say, "If the skipper gets a tin can someday, and I think he might, I'm going with him. That's the real war out there, on the destroyers and the escorts."

The others said they were happy to stay right where they were, on the tiny LCI, and hoped the skipper stayed there, too. I heard them say they were too small to attract a Jap torpedo, which made it easier to get some sleep. Another one said something about the only thing he worried about was the weather. With its special flat bottom for beach warfare, the LCI couldn't survive a typhoon. And typhoon season, they said, was just starting.

As life on the little transport settled into a routine, my spirits rose and then quickly started to fall. Without dwelling on it, I began to realize that I wasn't going to jump out of the rack and return to normal.

I couldn't even roll over yet. Or could I?

I pushed myself up in a half push-up, with no pain and nothing seemed to be tearing back there. I continued up to a full push up, hovered there awhile, then slowly lowered a shoulder and rolled over onto my side, then onto my back. Everything ached, and my muscles contracted and cramped hard down the sides of my back. That had never happened before. But everything seemed okay—odd feeling and stiff—but okay.

Heinz came in.

"Look at you. On your back. It usually takes a newborn baby four months to learn how to roll over. You did it in four days."

"Thanks, Heinz. It's all the breast feeding we did in officer candidate school."

"I thought OCS was pretty intense, seven days a week, round the clock."

"It was. We had to send out."

I asked him if I was ever going to meet the skipper. Heinz said Lt. Bayer had been down to look in on me every day, but I had been asleep. He also told me the captain wanted to know how I knew about the remains of the old rock pier back at the island. Anchoring on the submerged rocks had done the trick. It got the ship off the beach.

I didn't know how to answer that. And the effort to roll over had exhausted me. I closed my eyes and was soon sound asleep on my back. Heinz propped a pillow under my head and started to leave when the captain came in.

"How's he doing, Heinz?"

As Heinz explained my improving condition Navy Lt. Don Bayer of Detroit got his first look at my face.

"Zadoc."

"Do you know him, Sir? He was asking about you. Wanted to know if you were a TEKE from Detroit? At least I think that's what he said. What in God's name is a TEKE, Sir?"

Chapter Nine

This is the captain from the beach assault?
Yes, sir.
You sure he's a captain?
He speaks fluent captain.

***

I'd been sleeping deeply on my back. I opened my eyes and spent a half second orienting. The cramped bunk, the steel bulkheads—oh, the ship, the LCI, the injury. I looked around. Heinz was standing at the foot of the bunk. Over his shoulder was another face, an older man—dark hair, combed, a roman nose, a high forehead, and sun-roasted skin. He was smoking a pi . . .

Bayer.

"Zadoc! For cryin' out loud."

"Bayer? This is your ship?"

What followed was an elongated silence, during which young Heinz aged faster than his normal solar cycle. Unable to leave without pushing past his skipper, he stayed where he was, between the two officers.

Bayer ignored my question and continued with what he had been thinking.

"We need to get you transferred to a hospital ship, Captain."

Using the word "Captain" signaled to me that Bayer meant to treat me professionally and keep our personal history at arm's length. That seemed like a good idea to me, yet, for some reason it frosted my ego.

"Sooner the better, Lieutenant."

I put just a bit of foot pressure on "Lieutenant" even though a Navy Lieutenant and an Army Captain are the same rank. But Bayer felt it.

"Is he strong enough to handle a ship-to-ship transfer, Heinz?"

"Uh, no Sir. I don't believe so. He's still suppurating, and there's a fair amount of nerve damage that needs to be checked by an experienced surgeon. The only reason he seems to be comfortable is because he can't feel his legs."

"He'll be in a lot worse shape if we get caught in weather," Bayer said. And then added a bit of punch. "Or if we run into the Japs again."

Bayer looked at me, the third person they've been discussing.

"You have a bad injury. I'm sorry to see that. Our problem is getting you off this ship and onto something a lot bigger where they're equipped to help you. As you can tell, we're just too small. Anything that happens out here, it happens to everyone on board. We don't have a sick bay. The one we had we're using to store potatoes and rice. Normal routine. We'd signal that we have casualties on board and the Navy would send someone to get you, come hell or high water.

But there's something big going on somewhere, and we're not getting any help from Fleet. You may be stuck here a while. But your long-term health is at risk. Fortunately, we have Heinz. He's probably more of a doctor by now than any intern you'll see back in the States. What we don't have is medical equipment and proper sterilization stuff. We'll do the best we can. But be prepared. It's not a walk in the park at sea in any ship, especially one this size."

It wasn't the logic of what he was saying, or even the facts. It was the way he talked. You got the sense—why I don't know—that Bayer could handle things. It could have been wishful thinking. We were a small group of men on a very small ship in a very big war playing out on the biggest ocean on earth.

It's natural to hope that our guy has it under control. I admit I wanted to feel that way. And I did. It wasn't what Bayer said. He could have been looking for a cup of coffee. But his calm and his practical here-and-now personality fit our inner need for reassurance.

I gave into it as much as anyone. But deep in the left rear corner of my brain, I knew it was just a hope. I mean, the U.S. Navy in 1945 was a very big deal, but at heart it was just another institution, as was the Japanese Imperial Navy.

Institutions, strangely, are a bit like nature. There are good days and there are stormy days. Sometimes, the storms can kill you. Having grown up in institutions, I knew that no one ever really has it under control—ever. It's always an open issue. You just hope it doesn't get opened too much.

But then it did.

Chapter Ten

We're under attack.
We were under attack, he's gone.
That was just the first wave, goddammit.
Wave? It was just one airplane.

***

Clang! Clang! Clang!

One round glanced off the conning tower, but the other two penetrated the splinter shield protecting one of the ship's 20mm cannons on the starboard side of the top deck. The blast and the metal fragments severed Petty Officer Joe Romano's right arm at the shoulder.

For moments after the attack, while everyone in the con and pilot house reflexively crouched, waiting for another volley, Romano began bleeding out. The violent impact threw him down hard, ripping off one of his shoes, concussing his head on the deck and sprawling one leg, ankle shattered, straight up against a bulkhead. Thirty-five-year-old Romano, a burly man and the oldest seaman on the ship, didn't have long to live. His crew mates called him Little Joey.

The plane, a Kawanishi Shiden, nicknamed "George" by our guys, came screaming in toward the ship, just above the waves. It wasn't looking for the LCI; you knew damn well it wasn't. Nothing out here was looking for an LCI. It was escaping the fighting around Manila. But since Bayer's ship was in its path, the pilot squeezed off three of his precious, sausage-sized 20mm rounds before screaming overhead, just above the communications pole.

Below, the explosive rounds sounded even louder than they were, and everyone aboard felt the ship shudder and rock slightly. Chunks of steel clanged around in the well deck.

Lt. Watkins screamed down the companionway.

"We're under attack."

Captain Bayer called up the companionway for Battle Stations, such as they were on the LCI. When he got to the pilot house and looked around, he realized what had happened. The Jap, passing by, had squeezed off a few rounds in our direction.

Little ships like this didn't warrant precious ammunition. Bayer asked Watkins if he had called for damage reports. Watkins' blank face said he hadn't. Little Joey's blood started flowing past the pilot house. Bayer and Watkins and two seamen from the con lifted him out of the gun turret and carried him below, his arm dangling by a tendon.

They brought him in and laid him beside me. Blood spurted in pulses from a severed artery in Little Joey's arm, splashing across the room and across my legs.

Bayer spoke quietly, his face constricted.

"Save him, Heinz. You can do it."

Then he went back up to take command.

Heinz stood motionless for a second, then grabbed one of my unused pee towels and stuffed it against Little Joey's exposed shoulder.

"Get Vinnie," he told the two seamen, who ran out, glad to have a reason to leave.

Talking to me but really to himself, Heinz said that Vinnie was a machinist mate in the engine room who wanted to study medicine. He seemed to know a lot just from reading.

"Heinz, you can't stop an artery with a towel."

"I know that."

"Take the towel off and do a ligature."

"Serious?"

"Only way. Don't sweat the veins, just find the artery, pull it out a bit, and tie it off."

"Jesus Christ . . . it's squirting all over the place."

"Get a hold of it, you have to have more of it. Pull on it."

"Jesus Christ . . . I don't have anything to tie it off with."

"Just tie it in a granny knot."

"Holy shit . . . all right . . . all right."

By the time Vinnie arrived, Heinz and I had almost as much blood on us as Little Joey. But the artery had stopped bleeding.

"Get the kit, Vinnie, and start a transfusion. The captain here is Type O."

"Sorry, Sir. You're our favorite flavor, Type O. I'm going to have to use some of your blood to get Little Joey a few pints to get home on."

I didn't object. I couldn't get up and leave if I wanted to. And I wanted to. But I already had a pint or more of Little Joey's blood plastered on me. Least I could do.

As I tried to settle back and watch Vinnie's greasy hands prepare the transfusion, I thought about all the Japs who committed suicide when things went south. Maybe they were on to something.

Chapter Eleven

Zadoc, how in the hell did you know about ligatures?
Common knowledge.
I don't think so.
I read it in a Civil War book.
You read about it and knew how to do it?
It was the only book I had for four years.

***

"You helped Heinz save Little Joey's life."

Captain Bayer was leaning against the bulkhead, having a coffee. I now had a clean sheet over me, and my head propped up on a new pillow. Little Joey lay flat in the other bunk, still out, but Heinz said his blood pressure and breathing were stable, not normal, but stable. It had been three days since the George, the Jap fighter, had shot up the ship.

"We did what we had to do."

"How in the hell did you end up out here as an Infantry Captain?"

"I finished in the top of my class at OCS."

Bayer, still puzzled by finding me on board, asked how I knew about the old rock pier under the water.

I had no answer for him. I had no idea how I knew about the rock pier. I had never been there before. I had not seen any aerial reconnaissance photos—they didn't waste those valuable tools on Captains attacking islands you could practically pee across—and no one had briefed me about anything in the water. I did remember telling Heinz about the pier, but now, thinking about how I knew about it made me feel like two different people.

I told Bayer straight out that I just didn't know how I knew. And then I told him there is something else I know that I don't know how I know it. Bayer narrowed his eyes slightly and lowered his face just enough to say, "What?"

There's a storm coming. It's typhoon season, as I'm sure he knew. But I told him he had to top off his fuel tanks as quickly as he could. He had to be as heavy as possible before the storm hit.

Bayer smoked his pipe and said nothing. I'm sure he was thinking I must be nuts. I'd been wounded, paralyzed, so who knew what else was upside down in me? But then there was the rock pier. I had been right about that—and I was in worse shape when I brought that up. He smoked a bit more. I knew what he was going to say so I cut him off.

"I know what you're thinking. You've got to get Little Joey and me to a hospital ship and out of here. First priority. And I know you're thinking of dragging up and down the coast till you find one, or at least a bigger ship, to make the transfer. But things are popping all over the Pacific right now, and all the big stuff has moved on."

I was surprised that he just listened to me, didn't try to interrupt. So, I kept going.

"There's got to be a steady stream of the big boys flowing this way out of Ulithi. We need to intersect with that traffic and find an oiler. We might even find a hospital ship. That's my best thinking."

Now my eyes were opening wider as I watched his impassive face. Here was his hated old fraternity brother, an ex-con, and a lowly Army Captain, making an argument about something I could not have known much about.

Big stuff streaming out of Ulithi, hundreds of miles to our east? How did I know that? How did I know things were happening all over the Pacific? In those days, if you weren't involved in something, you didn't know about it—nothing, just rumors. Sometimes you didn't know much about what you were getting into even as you were getting into it. How did I know a storm was coming?

It all had to be too much to bear for a sane man, and Bayer was a pipe smoker. I didn't know myself. I didn't know anything, and yet I knew a lot. But let's be reasonable, this was nuts. I thought about saying just that. But what about the rock pier?

Finally, Bayer took the pipe out of his mouth.

"Are you sure that Civil War book was the only book you had for four years?"

Chapter Twelve

I'm having trouble holding the heading, sir.
Okay, turn into the wind, heading south southeast.
Is this just a big-ass storm, or are we in a real hurricane, sir?
We're in a typhoon.
What's a typhoon?
Kind of a big-ass hurricane.

***

The Captain, our Captain, did not heed my advice. We pulled into one small port after another, only to find that all the big stuff, the hospital ships and the big fighting ships, had all pulled out for operations elsewhere. And we passed up two chances to take on fuel while we searched for a hospital ship or an Army headquarters.

I had argued that ships survive better in heavy weather, that the oil and the weight, the ballast, of having full tanks was more important than my condition.

Twelve days at sea now, and Vinnie has welded a set of mop bucket wheels to the bottom of a straight back metal chair: my first wheelchair. I can move up and down the passageway, get myself to the latrine—sorry-head—and move in and out of the wardroom, such as it is. There's barely enough room in there for the three officers on board and a single Filipino, Isko, who seems to serve as both cook and steward for the officers.

But no one has gone near the wardroom for hours now, not since we got into the deep swells and the foaming breakers of a real typhoon.

Two Hours Later:

Isko, Watkins, and I are in the wardroom. I'm trying to hold a chart while Watkins gets his bearings. He throws up on the chart and stumbles to his quarters. Isko, who's been jabbering nonstop about the typhoon, something about his home wrecked by one as a boy in the Philippines, cleans up and then gets very quiet.

Ten Hours Later:

Bayer and one sailor are up in the con, a few steps above me. I've been trying to heat up a pot of coffee, and Bayer climbs down from time to time to take it up to the con.

Sixteen Hours Later:

Bayer, myself and Vinnie from the engine room are the only ones still functioning. The other twenty-two sailors, including Hennessey and Watkins, are puking in their bunks. The ship has been pounding, smacking its flat hull against a rock-hard sea, for hours now. Everything in the tiny galley that wasn't secured is now clattering around on the deck—flatware, bits of broken mugs, something that looks like a mixer handle. It's all covered in black, oily sea water an inch or two deep. I spent nearly an hour strapping poor—big—Little Joey to his bunk. Vinnie brought up a bunch of friction straps from the engine room. Little Joey is in pain, moaning over and over again, "Little Joey, Little Joey." He's bleeding again, not like before, but I can't do anything for him. Vinnie has been handling the six diesel engines for 20 hours straight. Bayer is up in the pilot house alone, I'm a few feet below him.

Eighteen Hours Later:

I stick my head out and call up the gangway to Bayer. We're rolling hard. Bayer is actually standing, for a moment, on what is normally a vertical bulkhead. He nods his head a couple times, okay. No point in even asking about the abandon ship drill. No one would make it over-board. Bayer, Vinnie and I have lifejackets on, but just to absorb some of the battering. Tanks crews and sailors learn how to ride their metal

33

horses without constantly smashing into all the steel around them. For me, without sea legs, or even legs, it's a rude assault that never lets up. I try relaxing and rolling and pitching with the ship. Blood runs from somewhere on my head. Is it coming out of my ears? My arms, which have to do triple duty for my rag-doll legs, are cramped and exhausted. I'm losing my grip, literally.

Twenty Hours Later:

The sky lightens the tiniest bit. I try to focus again.

Twenty-Two Hours Later:

The sky is brighter. The waves, the ones I can see, are no longer higher than the ship.

Twenty-Four Hours Later:

Bayer climbs down from the bridge. I got the stove lit and some old coffee reheated. He digs out a first aid kit, hands me a compress, and tells me to put it on top of my head.

"You were right," he says. "We should have taken on fuel."

He goes back up to the bridge.

Chapter Thirteen

"What the hell are those things?"
"Floating sea mines. We're in a goddamned minefield."
"What do we do?"
"Shoot them. They'll sink."
"What if they blow up?"
"Then we'll sink."

***

Thank God Vinnie kept the engines going, and Bayer stayed on his feet at the helm. The rest of the crew will now have to put an asterisk by their names when they call themselves sailors. LCI 797 survived the typhoon of 1945, and even I stayed on my feet, in a manner of speaking. It must have been especially hard for Vinnie—deep in the bowels of the ship, awash in fumes and oil. He endured a special kind of hell, I'm sure. And he must have known he didn't stand a chance of getting out, had we gone turtle.

I helped with coffee, moral support for Bayer, who had the helm for 33 hours—a bruising, terrifying 33 hours—and even pitched in with some dead reckoning. Navigation was my strong suit at Officer Candidate School. And to tell the truth—confess I should say—I made a few rum-smuggling trips on Lake Erie for my big-necked friends out on Nine Mile, back in Detroit. I don't want to talk about it.

But I know how to calculate drift, read a compass, estimate way (how fast a boat is moving on its course), and how to read a watch. Those are the basic elements of dead reckoning. Lt. Watkins, our hero left tackle from Notre Dame, was supposed to be Bayer's navigator. It was the only reason the United States Navy put him on board. Oh, sure, he was also second in command, but Hennessey could have come up from the engine room and done the job.

Word around the ship was that Watkins couldn't handle celestial navigation. I can't either. The Army doesn't take readings on sun or star angles using a sextant. Plotting those readings to figure out where a ship is requires some agile thumbing through tables and transferring the results on to a nautical chart.

Hennessey tells me that Bayer tried teaching Watkins from the time they left New York all the way down to the Panama Canal, all the way up to San Diego, and halfway across the Pacific. Watkins never caught on. Bayer finally gave up. No one knows how Watkins got signed off at Navigation School, but then, this was wartime. All the officers had little more than 90 days of training before they were turned loose in these tiny transports. Come to think of it, my own OCS training, from day one to brand new 2nd Lieutenant, lasted about 85 days. I wasn't even a 90-day wonder. Didn't matter. Even Isko, who had a couple years of college in the Philippines before the Japs showed up, and who had the polished manners of a man raised in an embassy (his parents worked for the British Consul), couldn't restrain himself from rolling his eyes when Watkins climbed on his horse.

And right now, Watkins was on his horse. He had the bridge. Bayer was sound asleep below. The sea was still rolling around like West Virginia, but the storm had passed. I was sitting in my wheeled chair, one arm locked around the deck rail, just outside the bridge house, sound asleep, lolling with the motion of the ship.

"What the hell are those?"

Watkins was leaning over the rail beside me, his face puzzled, but his voice had a hint of panic. It took me a couple seconds to focus.

"Sea mines. Full Stop. Or whatever you call it."

Watkins glanced at me, back at the mines. There were two, fifty yards off the port bow. Then another rose up in sight on a swell. And then another. Watkins yelled to the helm.

"Sea mines. Full Stop. Back Full."

The typhoon must have torn them loose. They're usually tethered just below the surface. The lookout on the con, just above the bridge, yelled down that he was receiving an emergency signal from another ship. He yelled down to Watkins:

"We're in a minefield, sir."

Watkins turned to me.

"We're in a minefield."

"I heard."

"Any ideas?"

"Yeah. Break out every rifle you have on board and start shooting them."

"Shoot them?"

"Shoot them full of holes. They'll sink."

"What if they blow up?"

"Then we'll sink."

It took me a precious minute to explain to Watkins how the mines worked. Reluctantly, no, it wasn't reluctance, he froze in place for a few seconds, faced with making a tough decision, and then he called general quarters and ordered every available sailor on deck. It took another perilous five minutes to break out the rifles and ammo—all locked up, of course.

To my surprise, the rifles were old WWI bolt-action Springfields. Heavy enough to do the job, but slow. Each three-round clip had to be loaded and the shell casing ejected manually. By now three of these menacing spiked balls were bobbing just twenty-five yards from our hull.

Seven sailors were lined up along the rail with their Springfields, but no one seemed anxious to fire the first shot. Watkins just stood there, squinting, in khakis and his faded Notre Dame football sweatshirt. I scooted closer to the sailor next to me and motioned that I wanted his rifle. I took it, chambered a round, and blasted the closest mine. I fired three rounds into it, just below the water line.

We watched, waited. Bubbles appeared around it. And slowly it sank out of sight. Now all the sailors opened up, a few of them missing the big target completely. As they blasted away, the sailors shed their sickly typhoon gloom. They chattered and cheered. I gave the old Springfield back to the sailor. One by one, the mines sank.

Bayer came up the gangway, carrying a cup of coffee and looking sleepy but a bit revived. Everyone stopped shooting. He sized up the situation.

"Keep shooting," he said.

He looked over the rail on all sides.

"Two sailors on the bow, two on the stern. Let's get a path out of here."

Watkins came over to the sailor next to me, took his rifle, and shouldered it in an awkward left hand stance. When he fired, he failed to anchor his cheek on the stock. The recoil kicked the bolt arm back and cut his lip. He handed the rifle back to the sailor, blood already dripping on his sacred Fighting Irish sweatshirt. He didn't say anything. Just squinted out to sea, and quietly went below.

Later, after we nursed our way out of the mines, I asked Bayer why the Navy had given him a navigator who didn't know how to navigate. Bayer, with just a trace of humor showing around his eyes, said, "He's my sister's husband."

Chapter Fourteen

"There's no facilities here anymore?"
"What do you mean? This is the biggest base out here."
"They're closing Ulithi. Everything is being torn down"
"What the hell? Why are they doing that?"
"You're to head back to San Diego."
"Why San Diego?"
"War's over. Japs gave up."

***

Little Joey died the next day. The big man had taken a battering during the typhoon. Heinz and I had strapped him to the bunk so he couldn't even move his head. But still, it must have been brutal. Heinz practically laid on top of him, trying to ease the violent pitching and pounding. Then Heinz got sick and crawled off to his own bunk below.

Little Joey had been improving, in better spirits just before the storm. After things calmed down, Heinz and Vinnie untied him, cleaned him up and brought him some broth and a chunk of stale bread. He sat up, drank, and chewed, and held forth with his first conversation since coming out of the fever or delirium or whatever happens to you when you lose an arm.

He was even better the next morning. He sat up by himself just as Heinz brought him some chow. He smiled at the sight of the food, said "Little Joey," kind of shouted it, with his big man voice. Then he closed his eyes and folded in on himself.

Dead.

Heinz said he'd read about this kind of thing, where a wounded person appears to get better, and then suddenly dies.

"It's a mystery," he said.

We were still five days out from making landfall at Ulithi, a big naval base protected by a huge ring of coral reefs—called a lagoon out here in the Pacific.

Heinz and Vinnie put Little Joey's body in a canvas bag, weighted it down with some used parts from the engine room, and with five other sailors helping, brought it up on deck. Bayer assembled the crew on the well deck and said some nice things about Little Joey, mainly about how he had been at sea serving the Navy long before war broke out. Serving, he said, when the rest of us could think of better things to do. He then picked up an old leather Bible to read, and this is when the unexpected happened.

Watkins, wearing clean khakis, stepped forward, and asked Bayer if he could do the reading. Bayer looked at him for a long second. We all looked at him. Satisfied that Watkins was serious—earnest—Bayer handed him the Bible. Watkins opened it, but I could tell he was just opening to a random page. He stepped forward and a couple feet to the right, in front of where Little Joey's head was beneath the American flag. The sailors had rigged up two planks of wood as a platform for the body. A third of the wood jutted out over the rail.

Watkins turned left and right and eyed the men, who were standing in two ranks at a distant resemblance of Parade Rest. The strange look on Watkins' face caused some of them to tighten up their military bearing. It was his eyes. They were saying something stern, and some of the men were hearing it. He then looked down at the prostate bulk of Little Joey and began to speak:

"Unto almighty God we commend the soul of Petty Officer Joseph Romano . . .

For five, maybe seven minutes, the sound of the sea against the hull and thrum from the engine room disappeared. All we heard was this transformed voice of Lt. Thomas Watkins. He spoke loudly, but not shouting, loud as in theatrical, and clear, and something else, a kind of pleasing resonance, the sound a human being makes when he's sure of who he is and where he stands and what he wants. For a moment, though, he got so wound up we weren't sure exactly what he was saying.

". . . And woe unto them that call evil good, and good evil, that put darkness for light, and light for darkness . . ."

I glanced over at Bayer, his forehead wrinkling, who was looking at Watkins, and some of the sailors were scanning the deck with their eyes. But then Watkins came back to earth.

". . . for into the deep we commit his body. But to you, God and eternity, we commit his soul . . ."

Watkins looked over at Bayer, who nodded to the Chief Petty Officer. Seven sailors lined up on the rail fired their Springfields, three rounds each. They didn't go off in unison, but it wasn't terrible.

Just before the service, the sailors had been trying to impress each other with their immunity to the seriousness of Little Joey's death. These young men, still just large boys, were jolted by the sight of a once-strong man turned inside out by dismemberment, and now death. They had been trying to calm their nerves by feigning amused detachment.

Watkins' performance brought them back to reality, back to the workday of war. This was a grim death, on a small ship, in a big war, on a vast ocean. The ceremony, brief as it was, seemed to calm them down. They all grew a bit taller, it seemed, if only a millimeter.

Watkins, of all people, had made it a human moment. And he had done it with the rough edge of the Old Testament.

Bayer gave a short benediction, and Vinnie and Heinz and four other sailors tilted the boards upward and Little Joey slipped off the wood and

41

dove toward the sea, feet first in his canvas burial bag. A couple of the sailors winced at the slight splash. Several of them looked aft to make sure the body wasn't floating on the surface.

We never made Ulithi on that trip. Bayer got a message that we had to return to the Philippines and ferry soldiers around. The battles there were mostly over, and soldiers had to be repositioned. We turned around, headed west southwest, found an oiler going our way, refueled, and went to work. While hooked up with the oiler, Bayer sent a dispatch to Fleet, letting them know that Petty Officer Romano had been killed in action and buried at sea.

We steamed up and down a million little channels between two million islands, picking up a few soldiers here, dropping off a few there. Occasionally, we took on board some battle-hardened Filipinos who had been waging guerrilla war against the Japs for more than three years.

This assignment dragged on for three months. Word was, we were staging for the big one: the invasion of mainland Japan.

During this island-hopping interlude, I took on the job of keeping track of where we were, the ship's unofficial navigator. Using my dead reckoning skills, I helped Bayer figure out where we were when the charts—drawn up by commercial traders in the 1930s—were vague, or just plain wrong. I even taught myself a bit of celestial navigation, and on a calm day with a clear sky, could get a fairly decent fix on a noon sun. That gave us a line on the chart. We knew we were probably somewhere on that line. I don't know how much this really helped, but it did wonders for me. When you have a big physical problem, like no legs, having some tough mental problems to work on is good medicine.

At one point, we pulled into a bay where some Navy brass had gone ashore to talk with an Army general. Bayer turned to me.

"That means there has to be a division level army medical group around here."

He sent Heinz and Vinnie ashore to see if they could take me. No go. The division, three divisions, in fact, were tearing down and getting ready to sail for the big one.

Heinz and Vinnie came back with a Navy Admiral in tow, a two-star fellow, called a Rear Admiral (you had to be there in 1800 or whenever they dreamed up the names for the ranks—probably the British). The big shot turned out to be a real guy, an insurance executive who had been in the Navy Reserve. He explained to us that everything was moving forward for the big one. He thought about it for several minutes. He said he noticed that our ship's bow doors didn't look right. This impressed Bayer, who later told me he had never met, until then, a senior officer who knew anything about these small LCIs. Bayer explained to him how the ship had been hit by a Jap tank, and the crew had done some emergency welding. The typhoon had broken the welds, and the bow doors weren't closing as tightly as they should.

The Admiral took a pencil out of his breast pocket and tapped it on his lips a couple times—some kind of a thinking thing. He probably did that back in his office in Hartford or Des Moines.

"All right. Steam back to Ulithi for repairs, and you can find a Navy hospital ship there for the Army Captain. Then, turn around and get back here on the double."

We pulled into Ulithi on August 15, 1945, now known as V-J Day.

Chapter Fifteen

What did the fleet doctors say about this?
Uh, nothing. You're the first doctor I've seen.
Who treated you?
Heinz. He's a corpsman on an LCI.
What's an LCI?

***

Peace can be hell. San Diego, where we landed, wasn't a zoo. It wasn't a mob scene. It wasn't a cluster drill. It was a human reenactment of the Big Bang. The entire Pacific Theater, free of the shoulder sag of war, suddenly came alive, took a collective deep breath, and tried to squeeze itself back into "God Bless America" through a city of 200,000 civilians and 2,000,000 service men and women. Or so it seemed.

But that wasn't the worst part. As we docked, well, parked, Bayer squeezed us into a parallel parking slot between two ships. The harbor master ran up and shouted at us to get the hell out of there. He screamed that we couldn't fit into such a small space, and that we should anchor in the bay. Bayer ignored him and neatly backed into the space. We were lucky to find a slot. Ships were already rafting ten and twelve deep at the wharves as the great stand-down picked up speed. Sailors on the last ship out on the raft had to crawl over all the other ships to get to the wharf. With no legs, that would have been a bummer for me.

As the crew went about shutting down and securing the ship—fervently hoping for the last time—a cheer went up on deck. Some family and girlfriends of the crew had found us and were running up the dock. The Chief had the crew duck below decks and quickly change into clean gear. Then he came over to Bayer, near where I was sitting:

"Sir, I think that's Little Joey's wife down there."

Turned out, the oiler we had left the casualty report with never got a chance to transmit word to Fleet. They were hit by a Kamikaze plane, which caught fire, exploded, and sank.

Mrs. Romano was waiting to see her husband, with her two-year old son in tow, "Little Joey," who had never seen his dad. Bayer went down the docking ramp to see her. The crew got word and slowly accumulated on the rail to watch the sad scene play out. Heinz went down with Bayer and came back to tell us.

"That's the Little Joey he kept talking about. He wasn't saying his own name, he was talking about his new son."

The crew was tongue tied.

"Jesus Christ," was about all they could muster.

Watkins then came alive and hurried down to join Bayer with Mrs. Romano. A wheelchair that a Navy Corpsman was bringing out for me arrived a couple minutes later, and Mrs. Romano collapsed into it. Watkins went with her and Little Joey and the corpsman. The Navy let them spend the night in their emergency room.

Then a typical snafu occurred that turned out to be an okay deal for me. The corpsman who took Mrs. Romano from the dock to the Navy hospital mentioned to someone who told someone, and on and on, until an ambulance showed up at our dockside. They had been dispatched to pick up an injured Captain.

An hour later, I was lying comfortably in a private hospital room normally reserved for flag level Navy officers, Captain and up. In the Army, that would be a full Colonel and up.

Figuring it wouldn't last long, I decided not to fight the flow. A nurse brought in fresh flowers, fresh food, and best of all, a fresh, American female smile. It had been more than two years for me.

After X-rays and some poking about, a Navy doctor, a Lieutenant Commander, a man two ranks below me, came in for "the chat."

"Sir, I'm surprised Fleet didn't try do a little mending on this right away. Might have helped restore some movement in the legs."

"All I can tell you Commander, is that it was hell on wheels out there for a while."

"Who attended you, Sir?"

"Dr. Heinz."

"Heinz? Don't think I know him. Well, straight skinny, Sir, at the moment, there's little we can do for you. But they are experimenting with some things, one is called microsurgery. If something pops, we'll find you and get you back in and see what we can do. Rest all you want, and when you're ready, we'll contact one of your aides and get you where you want to go."

"Thank you, Commander."

"If you give me your aide's name, Sir, we'll let him know when you're ready to sail."

"My aide? Uh, call Commander John Ma . . . no, he's on his way to Washington. Call my other aide, Lt. Bayer. He's visiting a buddy here in San Diego. They're on board LCI 797, right at the main dock."

"We'll take care of it. And I'll have someone here get you a set of Captain's blues and a change of underwear. What's an LCI, Sir?"

Chapter Sixteen

"Captain, your aide, Lt. Bayer, is downstairs in the lobby."
"Oh good. Send him right up."

***

Bayer, to his credit, figured out the game on the fly and played along. Thank God. It's not the official "trouble" I would have been in that worried me. At that moment, spirits were running high with the war over. I caught a glimpse of the nurses trying to do an impromptu *can can* in the hall one night. I don't think anyone would have dropped the Code of Conduct on my exposed little toe. And Bayer was in high humor. He had just signed over his ship, his cramped home for the last three plus years, to the Harbor Master, or someone official, without having to suffer through an inventory and inspection. Wartime protocols dissolve in peacetime victory.

What worried me was what was going to happen after he and I walked and wheeled out of the hospital lobby and into the bright and warm San Diego December sunshine. I had zero plans, no place to go, and I hadn't been in touch with the Army since my mini D-Day in the Philippines. It just recently struck me that I might be legally dead.

I think people go to war because it's so much simpler than peace.

We didn't quite make it out of the lobby entrance.

"Captain!"

A one-star admiral, a skinny, weather-beaten man with short white hair and brown liver spots, charged across the lobby and grabbed my right hand.

"I heard a little of your story, Captain. Leyte Gulf, right?"

"Well, north . . ."

"Captain, I just want to say one thing."

"Yes, sir."

His bony and painful grip still held my hand.

"We have watched many good men die. Those men died doing what we asked them to do, and in many cases a lot more than we asked of them. You and I and the senior Fleet cadre will live with that for rest of our lives. Do you understand me?"

"Yes, sir. I do."

"God bless you and get well."

"Thank you, sir."

He released my hand. Phew.

"Where are you headed now?"

My mind froze. I was still thinking about all those guys I left out there in the ocean. My aide came to my rescue. Bayer told him we were on our way to the railroad station. The captain, he said, was trying to get home to Detroit for Christmas.

"Take my car. It's right outside. Lt. Penn will take you right to the station. Tell her I said it was okay."

In the car, I thanked Bayer for showing up and playing his part. I didn't make a big deal out of it with Lt. Penn in the driver's seat. Bayer told me that he and Hennessey heard about my special situation when they came to the hospital to check on Vinnie. Seems that during the typhoon, when Vinnie was holding down the engine room alone for 30 hours or so, he got a pretty good dose of carbon monoxide poisoning. All the ventilation down there had been closed to prevent flooding, and every so often, waves overtook the stern and temporarily blocked the exhaust. During our last three or four months at sea, Hennessey had seen Vinnie become less talkative, slower moving. The doctors in San Diego said he would be all right after some special care, oxygen treatments, and so on.

But he wouldn't be all right.

Discharged honorably from the Navy with no visible disability, Vinnie went home to Montana. He bounced around in odd jobs and never made it to medical school. He died in his thirties, sitting on a torn, overstuffed chair in the basement of an elementary school. During his last three years, he had been the assistant janitor. His hands and face were black-smudged from feeding the school's coal fired boiler. But a small gold pin fastened at a bad angle on his frayed shirt collar still shined—probably from running his fingers over it as he sat there. It read, "USN."

The train station at San Diego was packed. Lt. Penn parked in a reserved spot and signaled for redcaps, who came running. Even with my wheelchair, we breezed through the crowd to near the front of the train and loaded into a converted dining car reserved for the brass. As we squirmed aboard, the redcaps carried me in the chair, Roman style, and Bayer gave me that "we could be shot for this" look. I told him they don't shoot cripples. I also told him that when we get aboard to tell the other officers in the car that I'm just coming out of shock from a tough operation. Don't talk to me.

We rode in comfort for three days, waited on by a steward. I'd aged a ton since that shrapnel tried to sever my spine. Still, I did my best to look like a bewildered four striper, mad at the world.

Chapter Seventeen

The doctor will see you now.
I don't want to see a doctor.
You're on a train traveling at night, right?
Meaning?
It's all slowly coming to the surface.
I don't believe that sort of thing.
Why didn't you just say, "Bullshit"?
Because I'm not quite sure who you are.

***

A strange thing did happen on the train to Detroit. It's mental, so it's not crystal clear, but that's not my fault. You don't know where the universe came from any more than I do.

Up to the hour Bayer and I boarded the train in San Diego, we'd still been fighting the war. In the service, when you're not fighting the actual enemy, you're always tangling with friendly enemies. I had to deal with the hospital as a fake Navy Captain, and Bayer had to deal with finding out how and with whom to get rid of his ship.

Try landing a crew of young men at a dock in blissful California after nearly three years of truffling sandy beaches for snot-nosed Japs and then telling them to bed down in their hot, ripe canvas bunks for a few more nights.

As we boarded the train and staked out our little kingdom at one end of the dining car, we were still in full officer mode. We were not celebrating victors eager to break open a bottle. You could hear a bit of a din from the jammed cattle car behind us, but that didn't last long. As the train started to move, and the hours and the landscape blended into a vague backdrop, the body began to relax. As darkness fell that first night, the comfortable rumble of the train allowed the brain to relax, too. That's when the trouble began.

My brain opened up in ways it had not for a long time, if ever. I became aware, slowly, of how frightened I had been the entire time—and maybe not just from "being at war." The safety and sanctuary of that wonderful, careworn train, that night ride away from the past, released every pent-up nerve I had. Like coming to inside an intensive care unit after an operation. Your eyes are open, and you're aware that you've been through something rough, but at the moment, all you can feel is the comfort of a specially heated warming blanket they just unfolded on you.

There, in the dark, I started to cry—silently, of course. I am a TKE. Bayer, on the easy chair across from me, was sound asleep. I hope. Losing my legs seemed to be at the top of the tear list. Close by was the months of preparation for war, becoming an infantry officer, fighting through imaginary battles, trying to remember what Clausewitz would have done.

But it ran a lot deeper than that. Losing my mom and dad and three sisters in the fire, going to reform school, getting chucked out of college, living in prison—all of it just poured out through my eyes.

And there was that damned admiral at the hospital.

"Men died doing what we ordered them to do. We will live with that for the rest of our lives."

Just what I needed to think about in the middle of the night while having one hell of a cry.

Women are right about crying. It does clear the insides a bit. By dawn, I felt lighter and healthier. I wouldn't say invigorated, but, okay, I will say it: I felt invigorated. By dawn, I began to feel so much better, I started to feel more like a navy captain again, and less like a lowly, crippled army captain.

The steward, a hard-pressed veteran of the line, brought our coffee at 7:10 and our breakfast at 7:30. As he placed our trays, and Bayer and I scooted into place to eat, I reminded the steward, in a flat, slightly worn navy captain's plaint, that, "coffee is supposed to be at Zero Seven Hundred, steward, not Zero Seven Ten."

Bayer gave me a "what the hell are you doing?" look. But I didn't care. I felt great. And boy was I hungry.

Chapter Eighteen

"Welcome home, Bucky Boy."
"Your father-in-law calls you Bucky Boy?"
"It was before the war. You had to be there."
"I can see that."

***

I wouldn't use the word "bond," mostly because I don't understand what it means, but Bayer and I had developed a mutual respect for each other, and I, more than a farthing of admiration for him. I thought he did his war well. I saw him worried a lot, but never panicked. Even during the typhoon, he seemed more grimly determined than frightened. And you could feel by the way the crew responded to him, with the oddball exception of Watkins, that they trusted him.

All groups of people—office workers, infantry soldiers, prison guards—tend to defer to the member of the group who is constantly thinking through the situation, the one who keeps the here and now and what's next at the front of his mind. Ship captains are supposed to be that person. Bayer seemed to fit the mold.

That typhoon, those long hours waiting for the end of your life, broke the frost between us in a way only a tropical storm can. For thirty long hours, it was Bayer at the helm, Vinnie on the engines, and me on the coffee pot. You cannot make this stuff up. After that day, and after I took over most of the navigation chores, Bayer and I worked side by side.

It was street ball, but sometimes street ball games turn into something bigger than playground ball. For those three months of island-hopping the Philippines, my dead reckoning skills allowed Bayer to concentrate on the rest of the ship. On the long slog back to San Diego, we spent hours in the wardroom, just the two of us, talking Navy, the war, some politics, and of our days back at good old Albion. By the time the train pulled into Detroit, we were really just two old fraternity brothers, home from the war. We weren't slobbering best buddies or anything like that, but we had shared a car at one time.

Our three days of rolling depressurization came to an abrupt halt just after midnight on December 23rd. Well, December 24th now. The train stuttered and halted at mammoth Michigan Central Station in downtown Detroit. Porters kindly huffed and grunted as they got me to the platform in my tired hospital wheelchair. Something was wrong. I saw vapor coming from my breath, and the metal frame of the wheelchair turned ice cold and started sucking the life out of my rear end. My first thought was "put me back on that wonderful smelly and warm train. I want to live there the rest of my life."

But the porters had silently moved on. Hundreds, I dunno, thousands of GI's and sailors slowly leaked out of the train cars, tried to find their legs in the cold air, shouldered their kit and quietly followed the crowd. Then suddenly, this tired black and white WWII scene turned into full color and springtime came running down the platform toward us in the form of a short gal, with curly bouncy blond hair, wearing a gray winter coat, saddle shoes, and a big smile. "Welcome home, Don," she said.

She gave Bayer a warm hug, and me, an incurable case of love at first sight.

She turned out to be Bayer's wife's sister, baby sister, Toni. While Bayer was introducing me to her, I felt the platform and my wheelchair warm up, almost instantly. I also caught sight of love's ever-present antidote, a tall, jut-jawed navy lieutenant in spotless blues—Toni's brand-new husband, Simon Hall. Overflowing with a potent mix of love and war's-over-ticker-tape-cheer, the wide-eyed couple had been dispatched to drive Bayer back to the family fold, a place called 39 Lincoln in the town of Mt. Clemens, about thirty miles north.

Bit of an odd moment followed, as Simon stuck out both hands to shake Bayer's one, saw my four yellow stripes and segued into a salute.

"Captain."

Bayer told him he'd sort it all out in the car. I saw Simon's handsome face furl in a "how do you sort out a navy captain in a wheelchair, and one who's coming with us?" look.

It wasn't till we got underway in their car, after the usual tussle with the wheelchair, that our new hosts learned they weren't dropping me off "along the way." I was going to 39 Lincoln with them. This caused only a slight dip in the conversation. Toni thought my short life as a navy captain had been a grand spoof. She said it must have been pretty crazy out there for an army captain to end up on a navy ship as a navy captain. I told her it had been "pretty crazy."

The roads were glazed with ice, and we zigzagged, sometimes almost broadside, toward our intended direction. Bayer sat in the front with Simon—apparently, they were old friends—and I had Toni to myself in the back, along with some of our sea kit. It was during one of these hair-raising skids that I realized Lt. Hall seemed to be enjoying the prospect of spending the night, if not the rest of his life, wrapped around a Michigan light pole. In the squash at the railroad station, I hadn't noticed that he had a pretty good buzz on.

As Simon pulled out of one swerve, oversteered and went right into another, he laughed.

"This is how we avoided Jap Zeros trying to strafe us in Washington."

Simon had spent the entire war in Washington, working on construction and supply contracts for the navy. Toni had been one of his secretaries. She turned to me with a tight-lipped, raised-eyebrow apology for Simon. At that same moment, while the car was still sideways, sliding down the dark road, Bayer looked over his shoulder at me, sitting behind Simon.

That look from him said something he would not have said aloud. From that moment on, there would be two World War II's: the one men fought and died in, and the one viewed from the safety of the home front.

So, I was wrong. Whatever our differences may have been, Bayer and I did have a silent bond. A strong one.

The houses were all dark on Lincoln Street in the Detroit suburb of Mt. Clemens. Except for 39 Lincoln. It looked like a hospital ship. A tall, two-story Victorian with ells and elbows and porches and windows and every light in every room, shining a welcome home from the war beams for Lt. Don Bayer.

I don't remember getting out of the car and up the outside stairs to the side kitchen door. People were everywhere, most of them in robes and night clothes. Toni's sister, Greta, who I quickly figured out was Mrs. Bayer, was the only one fully dressed besides us. She and Bayer quickly disappeared into the living room while Toni's other big sister, a tall redhead named Kris, put out her long arms and herded me, Toni and Simon, a handsome elderly couple—the parents—and a sleepy guy, named Coral (who turned out be Kris's husband), to stay where we were in the kitchen.

From there, we could see part of a magnificent blue spruce Christmas tree in front of bay windows. The tree, lit up in red and green lights and smothered with popcorn strings, took me back for a moment to a time before the fire. We used to have big Christmas trees, at least they seemed big to me as a small boy. Kris leaned her freckled face down to mine.

"Look under the tree. That's Don's three-year-old, Elizabeth, sound asleep. He's never seen her."

Chapter Nineteen

Isn't he the guy who stole your Packard at college?
He is.
And he's staying with you? With us? Over Christmas?
He doesn't have any place to go.
I'll tell him where to go.

***

39 Lincoln, as I quickly learned, was the very Germanic House of Hartmann. Father Hartmann, Ike to his wife and friends, raised his four children here in strict German patriarchy. Bayer later hinted to me that the family was a tiny bit slow in the late 1930s coming to realize Adolf Hitler might not be a good guy for Germany. There was some scuttlebutt about a local German restaurant the family favored that had been raided by the FBI during the war. Seems it might have been harboring a German spy, peeking in on the war factories around Detroit. I never got the full story.

For the most part, the Hartmanns were a handsome, even imposing, family. Father H looked the part. Square faced, blue eyes, and a full head of silver hair. He also had the charm of a gifted politician, which he was, locally, and had the keen edge of the fervently self-educated, which he was. Mother H, by comparison, seemed small, rounded and careworn, a woman who raised four kids in the teeth of the Great Depression. Yet, despite the worried look on her face, she had the unhurried head of a person used to having the last word.

Kris, the tall redhead, was the oldest. I would describe her as a live wire given to thinking out loud, punctuating her thoughts with laughter. I liked her instantly.

Then came a son, Martin. It took some time for me to understand that Martin wasn't somewhere else at the moment. The poor fellow had fallen asleep driving home late one night from school. He'd been away for months, learning to become a professional arborist. I had to ask, "Oh, like a tree surgeon, that sort of thing." He'd been hoping to surprise the family and join them for a short vacation. Ten years after his death, I think he had been in his early twenties, the pain still dampened family spirits.

Then came Greta, the least of the three Hartmann daughters in beauty, but by their own nomination, the brains of the brood. She reminded me of a stone sculpture from the who-knows-what period, when men wore robes. A chiseled Roman look, neither male nor female, but sort of penetrating, if that makes sense. A practical woman anxious to return her family, Don and their first-born, Elizabeth, to prewar routine. She was the first to sense that I seemed to be part of Bayer's wartime baggage, like some shrapnel men came home with and carried around with them for the rest of their lives.

Toni, the adult kid, provided the warmth and sparkle for the entire household. But her role as the baby seemed to have a maturing effect on her. In some ways, she seemed the oldest and wisest of the three.

All of this was my haze-covered fleeting impression. The warmth of a family hearth and home let all the steam out of me, and I sagged. I could have slept for a week. Except I couldn't.

I woke up early the next morning, jumped in my chair, scrubbed up a bit, and made my way to the kitchen. They had shifted Bayer and Greta and baby Elizabeth to an upstairs room and given me the prized first-floor guest room. It had been years since I had been in a home, one full of people, family people, and I wanted to take it in, all of it—especially on a Christmas morning.

I turned the corner into the kitchen at 6:30, and Mother Hartmann, in her robe and slippers, was already busy. She jumped a little when I rolled in, assuming something was wrong. I would have to get used to that. In the service, I was just another casualty. Among civilians, at least for a few years after the war, I was "Oh, you poor man."

When I said I was there to help make breakfast, she smiled in a way that made me think she didn't smile very often. Together, we made biscuits and eggs and bacon for the clan. A woman of few words, at least at first, she slowly opened up, I think in appreciation for my pitching in—–and from a wheelchair—while her adult daughters slept in like teenagers. We talked a little about the war back here on the home front, and she asked me a few questions about what it had been like "out there."

Just before the first of the family drifted in, Mother H abruptly stood stock-still and stared at me, commanding my complete attention.

"I have to tell you something."

"Yes."

"We're trying to give Don a good 24 hours of homecoming cheer before we tell him some difficult news."

Kris and Toni straggled in. But since they knew what was up, Mother Hartmann went on with her story. It seems that during the dark days of the Depression, and even into the earliest months of the war, a lot of families and businesses in the area had borrowed money from an insurance company in Detroit. This company came on the scene with tons of money and easy terms. The Hartmanns were among thousands who borrowed from them.

"The devil was in the details," Mother Hartmann said. "If you are late on just three payments, Nine Mile can foreclose on your property."

"Dad's in court right now, trying to save us from the vultures," said Toni, who still looked amazingly sunny wearing an old terrycloth bathrobe.

"I'm sorry, what is the name of this company?"

"Nine Mile Insurance," Toni said, scrunching her face. "Bunch of thugs."

Chapter Twenty

Is this "Big Dog"?

Who the hell is this?

This is Captain Zadoc of the U.S Navy, Chief. Just back from the Pacific.

Well, hello, Captain. Have we met?

You sent me upstate a few years ago for jacking a '31 Packard and using it to bring some refreshments in from Canada . . . you may not remember.

Well, I'll be goddamn.

***

"No."

Bayer spoke the word in a way that you knew any follow-up, explanatory, bigger picture, pros and cons, what could go wrongs, all we're doing here is, just hear me out on this—all that wasn't going to cut mustard with him. No way.

It was now the end of the second week in January. The historic flood tide of Homecoming-War's Over-Christmas-New Year's joy had given way to the quotidian concerns of checking tire pressures and paying bills. And figuring out how to keep 39 Lincoln out of the hands of the Nine Mile Insurance Company.

The facts were worse than we thought. Not only was Nine Mile foreclosing on Father Hartmann; they were after the town's municipal building, a nine-story affair, the largest building in town. They used it to lease space to pay for municipal services, like the water company and street maintenance. Turns out Father H, a member of the town's governing council, had borrowed against the building to raise money for some now forgotten make-work project during the worst years of the Depression. Now, the building *and* his political neck were on the line.

Bayer thought the navy captain gambit had been good, end-of-the-war fun, but not something that should be considered again, except as a good story at some 50th reunion. And then, he added, he wasn't fond of reunions.

The last two weeks had been the best of my life, with or without legs.

The family, the food, the banter, the good nature of these people who lived—and seemed to prosper—playing by life's current rules. I was enchanted. I even envied them a bit their Germanic intensity and Sunday piety. The only odd moment came during a dinner conversation beneath the elaborate chandelier in the Hartmanns' dining room.

Basically—and polite conversation seldom gets down to basics—the family wanted to know where I came from, and what I did after leaving good old Albion. You know, "What were you doing before the war?" kind of stuff. I told them how I had been orphaned by a house fire, taken in by a kindly aunt, who had since died (and she had, peacefully, I learned, while I was sailing about in the Pacific), and how, after Albion I had tried my hand in the wholesale business in Detroit for some large food chains, gave it up, moved to the Upper Peninsula, and pursued what I had been studying at school: social work, mostly helping young offenders in the state prison system (well, one young offender anyway).

"When did you steal Don's Packard?" Greta said, demolishing my theory of polite conversation.

"I didn't, actually. He wasn't using it much at school and I borrowed it to show off a bit with the wholesaler crowd."

"For two years?"

Instead of jumping in to help me, Bayer sat there near the end of the big table, smiling.

"Well, it wasn't . . . two years? I don't recall. I do recall I drove it back to Albion not long after I had it and found out that Don had left school after his dad's business went under. I eventually found him, but it took a while."

Toni then changed the direction of the conversation, and I let the loose ends of the story die with dessert. I know that Greta Bayer wanted to dig into all this and find out what really happened. But the bigger problem of losing 39 Lincoln and her father's reputation, and probably his job, kept the inquiry at bay—temporarily.

That was a week ago. Now, I wanted to do something about this Nine Mile Insurance company business. It had rat-hustle written all over it. And if my hunch was right, I might be able to tie up a few of those loose ends or at least cauterize them.

My idea was simple (I don't recall that I ever had a complicated idea):

Big Dog, who was now retired, would put on his uniform, I would put on my navy captain uniform, and we would drive over there and ask for a tour of the offices. We would tell them there had been some complaints about their business practices, and we would just like a quick walk-through. We would tell them that if they said, "no" we would quietly walk away. Naturally, such polite talk would make them think we were going to come back with a warrant.

"And what would a guy in a wheelchair in a navy captain's uniform have to do with this charade?" Bayer said.

"You know how civilians are; uniforms send a little shiver up their spine. Of course, there's the bigger reason for wearing it."

"Which is?"

"No captain's uniform, no retired chief of the Detroit police."

64

"I studied law in night school for a couple years before the war. This is not how you go about this."

"I've been studying law my whole life, from the inside. This is exactly how you do this."

Bayer was sitting on the outside steps to the kitchen door, and I was next to him, parked on one cement strip of the two-ribbon driveway in front of Father H's little garage. I could see his old buggy whip and wood-splitting maul hanging on the wall. It was one of those 50-degree days in January that feel like high summer.

Just then, Toni and Greta came out of the kitchen door with Kris. They scooped up Bayer and Toni and took my arm and squeezed it.

"We're taking Don out for a quick coffee and donut. You, you lucky guy, you get to go with us next time."

When they got back, Bayer looked at me and kind of sighed.

"All right," he said. "We'll try it your way."

Chapter Twenty-One

Well boys, I think we're barking up the wrong tree here. This looks like a well-run, reputable company. I didn't see anyone flinching or looking nervous—and I can smell a rat across a city block.

I thought so, too, Chief, until I asked them where the fiduciary department was.

They said they contract fiduciary services with another company.

Insurance companies don't have fiduciary departments—I made it up.

***

We drove down in two cars and kept it simple. Bayer and me in his old DeSoto, and the Chief in his new Hudson. I thought about it but decided not to ask Bayer what happened to the '31 Packard. As we drove along Nine Mile, I noticed a lot of changes since "my time" here. Small factories and warehouses had popped up, probably during the war.

The address for this Nine Mile Insurance company seemed to be close to where the big garage was, the one where we brought the booze in from Canada. But it was hard to tell with all the new buildings. My knees, mushy as they were, got a little weaker as we drove on.

And there it was, the big old garage. Only now it was painted white and phony window shutters and bushes had been added. The bushes weren't phony, they were real. The place looked pretty nice, but you could see it was just an old garage with false eyelashes.

"Jesus Christ, Bayer. This is the place."

"What place?"

"Where I used to work, during Prohibition."

"I thought you said you only made four or five trips to Canada."

"That was kind of a metaphor."

"What do you mean, if you go in there and they recognize you they might shoot you?"

"Not a chance. If you're not dressed the way people remember you, they never recognize you."

The Chief and Bayer boosted me up three cement steps and we entered a stale anteroom that opened on one side to a massive room where dozens of men and women, in ties and dresses, huddled over desks, lined up like a big parking lot.

"Looks like an insurance company from here," Bayer said, flatly.

The Chief shot him a stern look, reminding us about our game plan. He would do all the talking. A young woman, carrying a stack of mimeographs curled over one arm, walked by the opening, saw the Chief—or his uniform—and hurried off. A slightly older woman appeared.

"May I help you?"

The Chief removed his hat.

"We'd like to see the manager."

"Which manager?"

"The boss."

From where I was sitting in my wheelchair, I could see the ruffle of "the police are here!" working its way from desk to desk across the big room.

In short order, the management hierarchy appeared: first, a serious, thin young man with a pencil over one ear and rimless eyeglasses, then a stout white-haired woman with a pen on a chain around her neck, followed by the real boss: a middle-aged man in shirtsleeves with a stuffed pocket protector. All three wore that "what the hell is this all about?" frown. The boss waved his underlings away, and the Chief introduced himself with our agreed upon spiel.

"There have been complaints about your business, and all the fore-closures. We just dropped by to have a look around. We don't have a warrant. You don't have to let us in."

The boss didn't get it.

"You looking for one of my employees? Someone did something?"

The Chief tried again. This time the boss asked if we were here to "examine the books." Finally, he said, "You mean, you just want to walk around the building?"

"That's right," the Chief said, rather adroitly, I thought, "and if you're not comfortable with that, we'll leave."

The boss stumbled through a predictable sequence.

"No, yes, fine."

He slow-walked us up and down the aisles of the gymnasium-size old garage, pointing out the different departments, though they all looked identical to me. I kind of felt sorry for the guy. He just couldn't figure out what was up, and how could you blame him?

As he stretched out his arm toward each general cluster of desks, in-dicating what the employees did there—retail sales, commercial sales, underwriting, contract writing—he searched each of our faces for some kind of response. Bayer and the Chief ignored his plaintive face, but out of pure empathy I started giving him a quick "don't worry about it" head shake each time he pointed out another department. I didn't have a plan for this; it was just a human reflex.

But then we got to what he called the accounting department, another group of identical wooden desks all manned by women in the farthest corner of the building. As the boss waved his arm over the group and explained their job, I saw a face I instantly recognized—an attractive, quite short, middle-aged woman with black straight hair and a homespun look about her. I didn't know her name, and I had never talked to her, but I knew her. She was the woman who played the role of the tired young mother in the old Ford that followed me across the bridge from Canada. You never forget a face like that.

Without thinking about it, I nodded my head "yes" when the boss looked at me. He froze and stared at me. Bayer and the Chief turned and looked.

"Very important, the accounting department," I blurted, and I don't blurt easily. "You would be surprised at the troubles companies could avoid if they just paid a little more attention to this department."

That choice piece of whimsical nonsense didn't seem to clear the air for anyone, but the insurance company boss moved on to the next department. I looked back to see if the ersatz mother recognized me, but she didn't. Somehow, you just know.

Oddly, I began to feel that the boss had the idea that when he ran out of things to show us, something was going to happen, that we were going to arrest him or maybe shoot him if he stopped talking. He showed us the mimeograph, the coffee pot, and a little section of empty tables with salt and pepper shakers on them.

"I think we've seen enough," the Chief said.

The boss tensed.

"You haven't seen the mailroom and our storage area."

"That's all right, you've been very cooperative."

Then Bayer spoke up, quietly, as though he were, in fact, asking for information and not making a federal case.

"Where is your fiduciary department?"

"Fiduciary?"

"Yes."

"Well, it's not . . . we contract that out with a bigger company in Chicago. It saves us money, and it saves our customers money, too."

The boss examined Bayer's face to see if that was a satisfactory answer. Bayer gave him a reassuring nod.

Outside, the three of us clustered at the Chief's car for a minute. Bayer explained that insurance companies don't have fiduciary departments, and started to explain what it all meant, but the Chief cut him short. He said he could smell a rat a block away and this operation, to him, looked like an honest group of hard-working citizens.

"Did you see how everyone flinched when I got close to them? Real crooks don't flinch."

I decided not to bring up my bit about the woman in accounting. Bayer and I drove back to 39 Lincoln, pretty much in silence.

Chapter Twenty-Two

I don't get it. What did we do to cause these guys to cut and run?
Easy. We knocked quietly on the door of their guilty conscience.
I wouldn't think these fellows had much of a conscience.
Most of them know what the inside of a prison looks like.

***

I'm in the snowy backyard at 39 Lincoln. I'm babysitting Bayer's three-year-old, Elizabeth. I'm sorry, three-and-a-*half*-year-old; she corrected me earlier. The busy people around here picked up pretty quickly on the uses for a semi-stationary guy in a wheelchair. But this was better than my other silently elected job of lead dishwasher.

The week after our junior varsity Gestapo visit to Nine Mile Insurance was full of child's play.

"I didn't steal your daddy's car . . . where did you . . . I captured it. That's a whole different thing. Back then, I was a pirate. That's what pirates do. We capture things. You never heard of Peter Pan? What? That's right. I can't make a snow angel without legs, you clever little three-and-a-half-year-old. You figured that out on your own, did you?"

As I started to say, the week after we "visited" Nine Mile Insurance––and came up empty––was pretty quiet here at 39. The general feeling was, the game is up. Ma and Pa Hartmann were going to lose the family homestead, and, it seemed, all the memories . . .

"No, I can't make half a snow angel. Because if I get out of this wheelchair and down in the snow, I might not be able to get back up. The chair would slip away."

This big cloud, which no one wanted to look up at and talk about, was on everyone's mind. I think everyone felt that if they started talking it would all come out, so no one said much of anything. It was the quietest week I ever spent in close quarters with eight or nine people . . .

"You can't hold the chair for me. You're too small. You might slip and get hurt."

The thing was, everyone needed to get somewhere, and no one wanted to leave Ma and Pa Hartmann at this terrible time. So, there was this unspoken undercurrent of who was going to take care of the parents when they lost the house and their income.

Kris's husband, Carl, was already on his way back to their home in Racine, Wisconsin, where their two young daughters, Prudy and Peggy, were staying with his parents. During the week, Bayer told me he had just accepted a management position (why do managers have positions and not jobs?) at an insurance company in Pittsburgh. Obviously, they needed to get going. I admit I had to pretend to be happy for Bayer, as I was sure I would not be tagging along with him and Greta . . .

"Yes, that's a beautiful snow angel. But don't stay down there too long, you'll get your clothes wet and catch cold. What? I'm supposed to sound just like your mother, I'm the babysitter."

Bayer and I had talked briefly about my moving to Lewisburg, Pennsylvania, a small town in the center of the state. He had set his father up in a small hardware store there when the elder's big commercial laundry business got washed down the drain in the Depression. This struck me as a rather dreary option, but it had the advantage of being an honest job. With my background, even with my honorable war record—short as it was—I couldn't afford . . .

"I told you if you stayed down there too long in the snow, you'd get wet. Didn't I say that? Yes, I did."

Where was I? Toni and Simon, who were still fairly new newlyweds, (whatever that means), were looking for a house out on nearby Lake St. Clair. The point is, someone needed to step forward and offer a home for Ma and Pa Hartmann—a perennial issue for every generation, and everyone, including me, had spent the last week staring at our shoes. It wasn't the proudest moment in the history of the American family. Then something incredible, possibly incredulous, happened.

"If we go in now, I think we're going to stay in. I know, I know, you have to go, but by the time we get you out of that wet snow suit and everything . . . besides the sun has gone away, and it's getting chilly. How about if I make some cocoa and we search for Grandma's secret cookie jar? Good."

Nine Mile Insurance Company went up in flames, the whole building, right in the middle of the night. The fire company said it looked suspicious. The police said the company officers couldn't be found. One newspaper said the owners had left the state and didn't leave a forwarding address.

I said, "I told you so."

Bayer said, "I don't get it. You seem to know things."

Toni said, "Yippee."

And wonder of wonders, Greta came to me, smiled, and said, "You seem to be a good luck symbol with a bad luck background."

I took that as a supreme compliment.

Chapter Twenty-Three

Can two people in a wheelchair make a baby?

I assume you mean two people, each in his or her own wheelchair, as in two people who happen to be wheelchair-bound?

Spare me.

Medically, all other things being equal, I don't see why not.

I hate medicine, and I'm growing less fond of you.

***

Just before the perplexed euphoria of Nine Mile's midnight demise—and the sins of borrowing easy money were quietly repented—Bayer and I came close to having an adult conversation. Along the lines of what do you plan to do with your crippled life? What he really meant was, *am I going to tag along with him forever?* What he really really meant was *Greta wanted to know when I was leaving.*

Then Nine Mile goes up in smoke, saving the Hartmann bacon. I could see Bayer doing the addition: he knew about the stone dock at the Jap beach, he knew about ligatures, he knew about the typhoon, he knew what to do in the minefield, and now he pulls Nine Mile out of his hat . . . and my wife starts to like him.

I sensed that Bayer, a compassionate man by nature, was trying to figure a way to help me get back on my swollen and lifeless feet.

During that doleful week, when we were sure our Nine Mile adventure had failed, I watched Father H. He never flinched. Holding court each evening at the dining room table as we awaited the countdown to his financial ruin, he continued to speak in his acquired cadence of sympathetic royalty.

"How is my growing family tonight?"

Yet the only silver he ever owned was his thinning hair. The son of a Pittsburgh butcher, his station in life, the very house he lived in, were built on Mother's money. Her family owned a string of mineral-bath hotels during the days people came to Mt. Clemens for the cure. Father H had come for a hotel job and soon married up. But he was nobody's cliché. He had gifts you couldn't buy.

Perceptive, formal, articulate, he quietly swam ahead of the common fish. When people looked around the room for someone to explain what it meant, for someone to make a decision, for someone to point the way, their eyes turned toward Ike Hartmann. But for time and chance, he would have been some state's textbook governor. He never flinched.

In my three or four conversations with him since arriving at 39 Lincoln, he gave me the sense that he not only understood my tattered resume; he shared some of the pages. Bayer had told him about trying to get the LCI off the Jap beach.

"Sometimes," he said to me, without context, "it's up to us. We know where the rocks are buried."

At dinner the night after the Nine Mile cloud had lifted, Mother H prepared a pot roast and apple pie. All eyes turned to Father H. His dad-deacon composure was unchanged from the nights before.

"Let us hold hands, family, while we say grace."

While all this was going on, I'm proud to say I began to forge a small Mt. Clemens life of my own. It may seem small to you, but it felt large to me. It involved the young married lady living next door to 39. Until this rather late stage in my formative life, my relations with women had been (in this order) fleeting, furtive, sordid, and wonderful—*all* of them, few as there were.

I don't want to talk about them. But I do want to talk about Robin of West Tennessee, even though it ended badly. Mother H said she watched them move in just after Thanksgiving and the woman was in a wheel-chair, "like yours."

During the warm spell in January, which lasted just shy of two weeks, I wheeled across the Hartmann drive and theirs to chat with her. She sat three steps above me on the porch. Her husband, Octavio, a Georgia boy, had come north to work as a welder in a factory that made axles for Ford cars and trucks.

The first time you talk with someone, it's a pass-fail experience. She was wearing a navy watch cap, with auburn curls radiating from under, and seemed to be laughing to herself after watching me struggle to get the damn wheelchair through a few inches of snow and on to the dry sidewalk below her porch.

"What have we here? One of General Grant's supply wagons, trying to keep up with the cavalry?"

The second time you talk is story telling.

"I got meningitis at age 12. We'd been skinny-dipping in Crockett Creek—lots of that in West Tennessee in July—and the doctor had gone up to Nashville for a conference and some air conditioning. Octavio hates cold weather, and Yankees. But doesn't he love Yankee dollars? He got addicted working at the navy yards in New Jersey during the war. Can't think of one good thing to say about that state."

The third time is sharing intimacies.

"Octavio loves me to the moon, but I think he's disappointed we don't have kids. They told us we could try if we wanted to. There were seven in his family, five in mine, and now nieces and nephews are showing up like popcorn. I fear it's not enough for Octavio to spend his evenings listening to the radio or reading the Good Book. Now, tell me, where did you get shot? Can you still make a baby?"

The fourth is the beginning of a relationship.

"It would be terrible if two people in wheelchairs lived together, don't you think? We wouldn't be able to use the top half of the refrigerator or reach your hat on the top shelf of the hall closet. And what if one of us fell, what then? I don't even want to think about trying to make a baby."

I gave her Father H's old wood maul. I'd seen Octavio behind their house at night, chopping firewood in the orange light of their kitchen window. He was using an axe. Splitting bolt wood with an axe is tedious. The axe sticks most every time. With a nice fat maul, the pieces fly apart.

The next night, with all his extra firewood, Octavio overloaded their parlor wood stove and the house caught fire. He got Robin out but had a hard time of it. Carrying her in his arms through the smoke, he smashed her head, hard, in a doorway. When I left Mt. Clemens a few days later, she was still in the hospital, unconscious.

Chapter Twenty-Four

No, I was an army captain, not a navy captain.
No, I wasn't in charge of your son.
Yes, I was on his ship.
Well, it's a little hard to explain.
If I had to explain it, I would just say it was the war.
No, sir, not like the Great War, or the Spanish-American War.
Right, or the Civil War.

***

I'm sitting on a folding canvas chair, watching dust particles float in a narrow bit of sunlight between tall green pocket bins of machine and carriage bolts. I've been sitting here for three years. The canvas chair is a comforting break from my wheelchair, which is right here, too.

Welcome to the Store. You're the first customer we've seen today. We offer a combination of auto parts and accessories, a full line of hardware, from garden rakes to wall paint, and an inviting mix of seasonal diversions, from shotguns and bicycles to inflatable wading pools. We even have refrigerators and stoves, all with a full one-year warranty, including parts and labor. We have a bit of everything. We are the small-town answer to Macy's, a department store on one floor on a corner of a one-street, riverside college town, called Lewisburg, Pennsylvania.

What we don't have are very many customers.

Bayer has been in Pittsburgh for three years, climbing a corporate ladder at some insurance company. I've been here, halfway across the state with his aging dad, Father Bayer, trying to sell ladders.

Bayer set his dad up in this Store before he left for the war. Father B, wiped out by the Depression, had retreated into a deep one of his own. Working with him here in the Store for the last three years, he doesn't seem depressed to me, at least what they call clinically depressed. He just seems very Pennsylvania Dutch, which is what he is, a farm-raised descendant of Pennsylvania Germans. It's hard not to sympathize with what he's been through, at least until you get to know him.

He rode a horse-drawn wagon full of corn and vegetables right onto the Bucknell University campus in 1896, just a few blocks from here. He used the produce from the family hardscrabble farm to pay the tuition. In 1900, he rode out into the world as an accredited civil engineer, digging tunnels in the Alleghenies, laying out new streets for Atlanta. And by his own accounting, he was good at what he did.

Civil engineers are much like small town ministers. They have no choice but to work with the mess God has placed before them. If a mountain sits between you and the town's water supply, you have to drill a tunnel through the massif, and if you're good, you'll dig from both sides. If a trolley needs to turn a sharp corner, and at the same time, start climbing a hill, you have to get out your logarithm tables and patiently design tracks that bend correctly in two directions.

Bayer told me his dad's problem wasn't professionalism; it was misanthropy. He was right. In my three years living above the Store, and working here six days a week, I have watched one customer after another leave and not come back.

We have a 30-day return policy on nearly everything we sell—full refund, no questions—well, very few questions asked. Yet no one returns anything. They all seem to know about "the old man's temper."

I have spent days, weeks, months and now years pushing the vacuum cleaner up and down dreary aisles of car parts and hand tools, sucking up the ash dust that rises from the big coal-fired boiler in the basement.

I also made hand-printed signs for various sales: "Fishing Tackle 20% Off This Month," and tried, awkwardly, to make window displays using a broom handle to move things around beyond my reach from the wheelchair.

Father B doesn't do any of the artsy retail stuff. He tends to the business side of things. He opens the Store punctually at nine every morning, opens the big safe, gets the manual cash register set up, does the books, walks the deposits, such as they are, up the street to the bank, and makes out orders for next week's delivery. By early afternoon he is sound asleep at his desk in the back of the Store, his head back, mouth wide open. He is 79. He is sleeping there right now. The Great Depression was too great for him—as it was, I'm sure, for untold millions.

I'm afraid Bayer has left me with a problem I can't solve. The Store needs a major overhaul—starting with its sullen reputation—and I don't have the horsepower to do that, the first order of business being the politically delicate task of keeping the owner, Father B, away from the customers.

But how do you do that? Here's a man who has accomplished things neither I nor Bayer could, and who has landed in this low spot in the world late in life through no fault of his own, and now we have to tell him he's today's problem.

It would be like one of those historic cultures whose names I can never remember, nor could ever spell, that killed off their elderly when they became a burden. Or like one of those long-range patrols behind enemy lines and you break a leg. You know the unspoken rule. You get left behind but not to be taken alive. Out of false politeness, they'll let you pull the trigger, but you damn well better pull it.

While I'm frozen in time with this thinking, a customer comes in the front door. He is a tall, thin man in a dirty T-shirt, possibly a mechanic at the end of his workday. I stare at him. He has no face. It has been burned off. His nose and lips are completely gone. His teeth and gums sit out in the open. The rest of his face is blue-and-white scar tissue.

He says "Hi" in an odd, high-pitched voice, probably something to do with his missing nose, and without thinking I say, "You were on that oiler out of Ulithi that was hit by a Kamikaze and blew up."

He stops dead still, cocks his head a bit and says, "I was! How did you . . . were you out there, too?"

He points at my wheelchair.

"I was. We just refueled with you a day or two before."

"How did you know that was my oiler? Lots of oilers got blown up."

"Fleet. Someone at Fleet told me."

Sailors in the ranks rarely question something that comes down from the mythical heights of Fleet.

"Why would someone at Fleet tell you about me? Was it because we're both from around here?"

"Must have been. Must have been."

We had a good chat and I sold him some floor mats for a '47 Ford four-door sedan.

At a quarter to six, just before closing, the side door of the store opens, the door used mostly by salesmen and old chums of Father B. A woman in her 40s enters, wearing a schoolteacher dress and a quizzical look. She immediately peers down the first aisle toward Father B's desk and sees him sound asleep. She seems to know the place. She turns back in my direction, toward the front desk, smiles and extends her hand.

"You must be Zadoc. I'm Dorothy Watkins. You were on Don's ship with my husband, Tom. We just moved back from California. That's my dad, sound asleep back there."

"Lieutenant Watkins?"

"Reverend Watkins now."

Chapter Twenty-Five

I understand Tom helped Donald get safely through the war.
He did. If it hadn't been for old Tom, we'd probably still be out there
wandering around the Philippines—or at the bottom of the Pacific.
Tom was a rare officer.

***

For the first time in all these years, I've been invited to Father B's large Victorian. It's just a few blocks from the Store, but in a shady lane of turn-of-the-century homes.

The momentous event is a dinner party for their daughter, Dorothy. She teaches home economics at the high school level and knows how to cook. Mother B and Father B, by dint of their inherited natures, or possibly because of some shared apocalyptic event, do not entertain, seemingly, even themselves. They also don't seem to talk to each other.

Mother B has not been to the Store in my three years there. I wonder if she has a driver's license. It's 1949, and the two strike me as people from another century, another time, which they are of course. It briefly crosses my mind that the 19th century, with its horses and carriages and wing collars and bustles and bowlers, must have been hard to let go of. But I think they both came from farms. So, forget about missing the bowlers and bustles.

We're seated at a large rectangular dining room table, auspiciously located in a dedicated dining room, outfitted properly with service sideboards, huge, heavy maple sliding doors for guests, leading to a sitting parlor that leads to another sitting parlor, and a silently hinged door to the kitchen for the service staff, which tonight is Dorothy.

I'm seated in my trusty wheelchair at the 50-yard line, on the visitor's side, away from the sideboards. Mother and Father B occupy opposing end zones, and the table settings for Tom and Dorothy are opposite me, at about the 40-yard line. If everyone looks straight ahead, only Father and Mother B would be able to see eye to eye, and I sense they can't or don't care to focus at such a distance.

There is a multi-tiered chandelier hovering over the table—not that different from the one in the Hartmanns' dining room in Michigan. I wonder if it ever occurred to Bayer that when you come from chandelier you tend to marry chandelier.

Dinner is roast chicken, mashed potatoes, peas, and store-bought yeast rolls. Dorothy insists we start, even though Reverend Lieutenant Watkins hasn't arrived. I'm surprised when she shares some news.

"Tom is on his way from California. He should be along any time now. He'll be surprised to see you here. He doesn't know you've been working with Dad all this time. I didn't know either till I talked with Donald yesterday in Pittsburgh."

Mother B's head movements showed she was hard of hearing

"What's that?" she said.

"Mr. Zadoc here is not just a hired hand at the Store."

"He's not?"

No wonder I've never been invited for Thanksgiving leftovers.

"He is one of Donald's officers from the war. They were together on his ship in the Pacific. He's a friend of Donald's from college."

"Well, for heaven's sake."

Mother B now looks at me straight on for the first time, smiles, and extends the small platter of rapidly cooling yeast rolls. I look over at Father B. He has known who I am since the day Bayer delivered me to Lewisburg three years ago, though we haven't discussed the war since my first few days working with him.

He is chewing and staring off at infinity with no flicker of recognition that this bit of conversation has revealed a household misapprehension.

"You must be anxious to see Tom again, too," Dorothy says. "When he saved the ship in that storm and got it out of the minefield, he saved your life, too."

For a second, I thought about just chewing and staring into infinity, but you can't just do that at the drop of a hat. It takes practice and certain talents.

"Indeed, I am looking forward to seeing him again."

I wondered if Wandering Watkins the Navigator thought that he'd never run into his brother-in-law when he made up his war stories. Maybe he had a drinking problem, or worse. Maybe he really believed what he told his wife. Or maybe it was just the bitter taste of war, and this was how he was getting it out of his mouth. Hard to hold that against any man or woman who has been there.

We had apple pie and vanilla ice cream for dessert. Fortunately, for Tom, his journey from California suffered some delays, and he didn't arrive until long after dinner, and I had left.

The following Monday morning, Bayer called me at the Store. He had quit his job and was moving to Lewisburg to take over the Store. I woke up Father B to relay the news.

"Well, for cryin' out loud," he grumbled.

I couldn't tell from that whether he was pleased or not.

Chapter Twenty-Six

How do you get up and down all those stairs?

There's a freight elevator in the back of the Store.

But then you have to cross the roof in the open to get to your apartment.

I do, rain or shine.

What do you do when it snows?

Wait for Spring.

Seriously.

Bobby Spring, kid we hire to shovel the sidewalks in winter.

***

For the past three years, my personal life centered around a freight elevator whose insides had been dented, warped, and rubbed raw by the goods it moved up and down the warehouse at the back of the Store. I nicknamed it "Fretty."

You can't bring a date to a freight elevator, at least not a first date. You can bring propositions aboard Fretty, but that goes without saying. And I'm not . . . saying. City girls in loft neighborhoods may or may not ride freight; small town girls do not. Think about how the stage directions would read:

Couple lingers over after-dinner drinks.

Couple walks and wheels to front door of Store.

Couple enters Store, turns on all the lights.

Female flinches a little as male locks front door behind her.

Couple slowly make their way through eerily silent hardware to back of Store.

Female's eyes widen as they enter dusty, slightly trashy warehouse.

Female begins silently rehearsing unworkable escape plan as male opens battered gate to freight elevator with one-naked lightbulb.

Female now realizes her mother was in fact a forward-thinking prescient genius and not a leftover relic from another time.

Female rapidly reviews escape scenarios:

A. Left purse—her other purse—at restaurant.

B. Left keys in car.

C. Forgot her sister's getting married tomorrow and must rush home to fit a dress.

Female choses a creative combination of B and C, i.e., she left her sister in the car without keys, calculating (correctly) that the improbable is more believable.

Female asks if there is a door to the Store that meets fire code regulations: you can open from the inside while it is locked to the outside.

Male, who now fully understands the game is being called before the sixth inning, says "Yes, on the side street, in tires and hubcaps. I'll show you."

Female says she'll have no trouble finding tires and hubcaps.

End of evening.

And then Skyler, with her long jean skirts and puffy white blouses, moved in across the dingy hall from me on top of the Store. I didn't realize there was a habitable apartment there to move into. Father B used that space to store all the paperwork needed to run the Store, order books, stationery, catalogs, big green ledger books stacked like cord wood, receipt books, three-hole binders with hardware and auto-parts manuals, outdated promotional flyers—enough evidentially to fill what I now realized was an apartment just large enough for one human being, assuming the cloistered renter didn't make any sudden or wide-reaching moves.

Since we slept with our heads a mere four or five feet apart, we got to know each other in about eighteen hours. Standing in our little galley kitchens, we could open our grimy hallway windows and pass milk and butter back and forth. But the ice really broke when I showed her how to use Fretty to bring her heavy bike upstairs. That's when she told me she had been an orphan from age ten, graduated from Albion two years behind me, and now was going back, in her early thirties, to earn a Master's in Literature at Bucknell.

I swooned—or at least went through the range of feelings I think swooning causes.

"I'm an orphan, I went to Albion."

We were standing in Fretty. She fixed me with large brown eyes that would melt a snowman (when you are swooning, you say such things).

"What about the Master's in Lit?"

I swung:

"Jane Austen . . . *Pride and Prejudice, Sense and Sensibility, Emma, Mansfield Park, Northanger Abbey* . . ." That was it. I was out of ammo. And I only had that because I found them in my cell in the Upper Peninsula.

The muscles in Skyler's gentle round face softened and she smiled. For the next two years, we had dinner together most nights, worked crossword puzzles on Sunday afternoons, went wheel-chairing and walking on the quiet streets of town, and on cold winter nights took turns reading aloud all of Jane Austen, with me trying vainly to defend Wickham and Willoughby. We laughed about things I can't recall, little things.

At Christmas, we overdecorated our miniature apartments with whatever hadn't sold from the Store. And one Thanksgiving, we got so engrossed in our discussion of Lady Catherine de Bourgh that we burned our little roast chicken and had to scramble up the street for hoagies before the shop closed.

And then she got her master's and left to make her way as a professor. I woke up some time later and looked across the hall. All the boxes of daily receipts and stacks of ledger books were back again, collecting dust.

Chapter Twenty-Seven

Don't worry about it. Your credit's good here.

What if I move out of the area and never pay my bill?

I'm not worried. I have three cousins in New Jersey, the kind who wear suits and ties to the beach.

I was just kidding.

I was, too. They never go to the beach.

***

Bayer and Greta moved to Lewisburg, now with three kids, two girls and a boy, and everything changed. The bank, Bayer said, had called him in Pittsburgh. The Store had been running on credit for six months. Something had to change, or they would pull the plug.

First thing we did was move Father B further toward the back of the Store. This was accomplished in a cloud of Pennsylvania Dutch obscenities, that translated, didn't sound so terrible: "donnerwetter" equals "thunder weather."

Then we began a year-long campaign to overhaul the entire Store: new tiled floor, new display cabinets and shelving, new lighting, and a fresh coat of paint on everything. We did this ourselves, except for some electrical work, closing at six and laboring till ten or eleven every night and Sunday afternoons. 'Course, Bayer did most of the work, while I gofered and painted areas I could reach.

All this after-hours activity stirred up a frisson of curiosity. Benjamin Franklin used to scurry around the streets of Philadelphia with armloads of flyers just to make people think he was a busy printer. More of our customers came in after hours than during the day. We stopped and politely sold them our hardware and auto parts. They seemed energized meeting Bayer, a man of their age and time. Some still peered toward the rear of the Store to see if the old lion was still there. Mr. Leonard, a wiry, hyperactive man who managed the small grocery next door, dropped in, wearing his vegetable sorting apron. He didn't say much— didn't have time to chat. Just a nod, and "Good work, men."

The second big thing we did was open a credit file folder for anyone who didn't have enough money just then—no questions asked. We picked up some duds, naturally. Word about easy credit takes less than a month to filter through a town of about 5,000 postwar families, trying to sort things out and build new lives. A lot of veterans streamed in to buy new tires on credit, then farmers, some with barn mud still on their boots, then schoolteachers, nurses from the town hospital, and a long line of mill workers from the town's big furniture factory.

Business boomed.

Oddly, like our time at sea in the LCI, Bayer and I didn't talk much, outside of immediate business, even as we labored side by side. In a way, he hadn't changed from his days as a wartime Navy skipper: quiet, efficient, pushing forward. But I could tell the move to Lewisburg, leaving a promising corporate career for a failing auto-parts store in small-town America, had to have him worried.

Greta, who now loved me for saving her family—or seeming to have saved her family—had me over for dinner on Saturdays. Bayer had bought an old Ford pickup for the Store and had it fitted with crude hand controls. It more or less became my truck.

The big advantage for everyone is I didn't have to be freighted about town anymore. After we closed on Saturdays, I drove to their house. Their small, wood-frame starter home, clad in drab asbestos shingles, sat on a dead-end street just a couple blocks from Father B's big Victorian. The contrast stood out now and then in the way Greta referred to anything about her in-laws: she didn't care for them. I never found out why, but there was obviously a bit of less-than-genial history in play. I assumed she didn't think much of Bayer leaving a middle-management job in the city to take charge of a small-town auto parts store in bad need of repairs.

We were sitting at their kitchen table, over coffee. The murmuring upstairs from their three children had died down. It had been another long week trying to breathe life into the Store. Bayer looked tired but relaxed; Greta, poised and earnest. She turned to me.

"I don't understand. Why are you working at the Store all these years, and for no pay?"

"I have my disability pension from the VA, and I get to live free above the Store."

"In that dinky apartment . . ."

"I like to think of it as the pinthouse penthouse."

"What about your friends?"

"Friends?"

"Girlfriend?"

"Oh, Skyler. She got her master's and now teaches at a small college in Arkansas or Missouri or someplace like that."

"Which college?"

"I think it's called Stephens."

"Stephens?"

Bayer joined in.

"He knows things. He can see the future . . . back during the war . . ."

"I know, I've heard the stories. Do you know if we're going to put our three kids through college with this Store?"

She said the word "Store" as though it were a question mark all by itself.

"Well, I do."

"And?"

"The answer is yes and no. You will be able to put the kids through college. But it won't be three kids."

"Meaning?"

"It will be four kids."

Bayer smiled. Greta didn't buy it.

"Did your crystal ball tell you why Don left a very good paying job in Pittsburgh?"

"To bail out his father. I don't know."

"You know things, but you don't know this. A company called Nine Mile Trust . . ."

"Our old friends," Bayer said.

"They bought Don's company and then fired him—the only manager they fired, far as we know," Greta said. "And then they blackballed him in the insurance industry."

"Oops."

"Oops, indeed."

Chapter Twenty-Eight

I thought I was a foreseer.

You are.

Then why didn't I foresee Nine Mile sandbagging Bayer in Pittsburgh?

Well, I guess you're not one of the all-time great foreseers.

Oh.

***

Clearly—I use the word "clearly" because it gives the impression that I know what the hell is going on—attaching myself to this enviable American family without contaminating them with my unenviable past wasn't working well. It wasn't just the foggy miscreants from Nine Mile. It was my peculiar affinity for such people and their ilk.

At least that's the way I felt—at the moment. But at the same time, I had foreseen all of this . . . well, not everything; foreseers aren't any more perfect than you are. So, let's just climb down from that horse while I figure this out.

At the Store, the day after the "Did you know?" dinner, I asked Bayer about it point blank. He took his bent pipe out of his mouth and smiled. Say what?

"I'm not unhappy about it," he said, as the corporate litotes in his blood prevented him from being too direct. But then he caught himself and moved all the way into the countryside where the rest of us now lived.

"It gives me a chance to solve Dad's problem and be my own boss. Corporate life has its rewards, but they wear thin after a while."

He tapped his pipe in his palm a couple times and looked around the Store. He didn't want to go into it any more than that. Clearly.

We went back to work. It took a few years, but the ten to fifteen customers we counted daily grew to twenty and then twenty-five—good but not the stuff that gets you on the cover of *Hardware Age* magazine. Even so, every time the little silver bells over the front door jingled, I looked up to see if it might be a Nine Mile creature looking for trouble. But it was always a customer looking for someone to talk to. Customers come in the first time because they need something, or they are just looking around. They come in the second time because they found someone who will listen to their troubles.

Farmer Gordon came in. A regular, he always had God on his mind. And he wanted me to have God on my mind, too. Standing tall in his pungent muck boots, he put his purchase under his arm and looked down at me across the checkout desk, trying to freeze me in place with eerie, electric blue eyes.

His voice went up a decibel.

"Fear of the Lord, son, is the beginning of wisdom."

I had been prepping for this.

"Simon loved Jesus as a friend before he loved him as the son of God."

I could tell from the way he blinked and slightly raised his chin that I had returned his serve with a little mustard on it.

I charged the net.

"I'm talking about Simon, son of Jonah, not the other Simon, the Canaanite, St. Simon the Zealot. Simon, the one called Peter, the rock upon which Christ built the Church. So sayeth the book of Matthew."

Farmer Gordon, who was either on a tight deadline back at the farm, or had broken a string in his racquet, maneuvered around to the side door.

"In the name of God, son. In the name of God."

And he was gone. An hour later, a living Simon came in. Simon Hall of Michigan. I didn't recognize him. He was dressed to call a New York City cab to the curb, in a dark suit, white shirt, and silk tie. But when he smiled and extended his hand, I got it: Toni's husband!

Unfortunately, Toni wasn't along on this trip. Simon was driving to Baltimore on family business. He had just stopped in to say hello and be on his way. He chatted with Bayer and me for about forty-five minutes. And those minutes turned out to be golden for us. After looking around the Store, he made three suggestions we might want to try.

First, we should put items that make life fun, or easier, in the windows: hunting gear, the new line of self-defrosting freezers. Second, make the front half of the Store well organized and seasonal: bicycles and lawnmowers in summer; snow shovels, antifreeze, and boots in winter. And finally, he said we should "junk up" the back half of the Store.

"People love to dig through piles of goods. Makes them feel as though they found a bargain, even if it's a rather pricey item."

I was thinking, "Sure, Simon. Is this something you learned during the war, riding a desk in Washington?" But Bayer was really listening to him, so for once I kept my mouth shut. But then I opened it.

"Where did you learn all this?"

"I wrote a thesis on small retail at school."

"What school?"

Why is Bayer smiling?

"Wharton."

"Oh. Were you a TKE there?

"Sigma Chi."

After he left, Bayer told me that Simon had grown up living above a family corner street bodega in a seedy part of Baltimore and got a scholarship to the big deal Wharton School of Business at the University of Pennsylvania.

"Funny, I could have sworn he was a supercilious clown."

"Well, you did hear what he said."

"What?"

"A Sigma Chi man."

Again, it took us awhile—nothing happens too quickly in a small store—but we gradually did everything Simon suggested. Our twenty-five customers grew to nearly forty a day, and on Fridays and Saturdays we started to see fifty. With a Christmas holiday approaching, we loaded up on train sets, play kitchens, and dolls. We built a miniature village, complete with working streetlights and put it in the window with a realistic looking American Flyer train that circled the village from nine a.m. till nine at night.

The queues at the front cash register got too long, so we scrambled around and found a cheap box cash register used at county fairs and installed it on Father B's desk toward the back of the Store.

"Well for cryin' out loud."

And we moved him, gingerly, to a tiny platform way in the back, a place normally used to assemble bikes and toys. The rest of Father B's big desk became our gift-wrapping station. It wasn't beautiful bow wrapping, like from Macy's Department store in New York City, but we had nice, Christmassy paper and tons of scotch tape.

We also had, to my delighted surprise, our own private army of gift wrappers. Every day after lunch in the final nine-to-nine week before Christmas, Bayer's three kids came in to man the wrapping table. The little one, twelve-year-old Margot, dispensed the scotch tape; thirteen-year-old Chase manned the big paper roll, and meticulous Elizabeth, now fifteen, did the wrapping. The results didn't win any prizes, but the customers loved it.

Suddenly, we had a hair-raising number of customers. A huge snow-storm, twenty-seven-inches worth, cancelled anyone's idea of traveling twenty miles to the nearest city for last minute upscale shopping.

That Christmas eve, we had customers lined up on the cold, dark, and snow-covered sidewalks, waiting to push in for a chance to buy whatever we had left. Mixed among our regular crowd of farmers and factory workers was a good swath of the town's cardigan-clad lawyers, doctors, and Bucknell profs—men and a few women who rarely bought from us, save for a dead car battery or a screwdriver for a weekend project.

Tonight, they had enough packages in the arms that you couldn't see their faces as they wiggled their way from the checkout desk to the front door.

One lady, rather short, wearing a black fur coat, seemed to be carrying more than I thought she could handle.

"Do you want one of the kids to help you with some of that?"

She quarter-turned to me. I couldn't see her face, just her profile.

"No thanks. Car's right outside."

She didn't say "caar" like a Pennsylvanian. She said, "karr," with a strong Michigan, Detroit area, accent.

Then it hit me.

"You're the mother from Nine Mile."

I hadn't meant to say it out loud. At least I don't think I did.

She dropped her packages on a display case near the front of the Store and was gone.

I asked young Elizabeth if she could man the cash register for a minute and started rolling through the crowded aisle toward the front door. It was thirty minutes to closing and there were still people coming in, including a woman in a wheelchair. I had to pull up so she could roll by me, but she stopped right in front of me.

"Merry Christmas, Yank."

"Robin?"

Chapter Twenty-Nine

Nine Mile in Lewisburg?
Doesn't make any sense.
Robin's in Lewisburg?
That certainly doesn't make any sense.
I don't get it.
You don't get it because it doesn't make any sense.
I got that.

***

It's hard to explain how good you feel while being nearly flat-on-your-face tired after three weeks of a nine-to-nine Christmas crush. Our Store, Bayer's Store, was the center of our corner of the world just then. I was happy and numb—and now I was anxious. It was almost nine p.m. We were minutes from wrapping up our best season ever. And we still had a long but happy night ahead of us.

For the last several years, I've lost track exactly, the end of business at the Store on Christmas Eve marked the beginning of Christmas Eve with Greta and Bayer. After locking the doors, Bayer and I would spend two or three hours wrapping the children's gifts. While Greta, at home, got the kids into bed and settled—two distinct operations—we put all the gifts in the back of the truck, and piled in the family Christmas tree, which we had been hiding in the warehouse. Their family tradition had the tree appearing magically on Christmas morning.

But this was usually just the beginning of the night. One Eve, we worked most of the night after closing the Store, building a special platform with a train set and Christmas village, and mounted the tree in the center. Another year, we finished building a full-size ping pong table. Sometimes, bicycles and wagons had to be assembled. And always, there was a tumbling, overflowing hill of presents, flooding out from the Christmas tree and spreading across their living room floor. We never talked about it, as we drank coffee and munched on Greta's cookies till three in the morning, but we were wiping out the darker moments of holidays growing up in the Depression.

Without trying, I had spent most of my life to this point avoiding sentimental moments. Growing up in a boys' home, and then prison, you do this to protect your guts. You don't think about *how* to do it, you just do it. It's like teaching a kid how to do a flip off the low diving board. You don't start with some prattle about kinetics; you tell him to get up there and just do it. And he does.

Now though, and over more than a dozen Christmas Eves and mornings—once I slept over on the couch, surrounded by presents and the scent of the spruce tree—I began to see, and more dramatically, feel what the holiday meant to Bayer's (now) four children.

I was asleep under a thick sandwich of blankets when the kids came downstairs to behold the power of human warmth–the tree, the presents, the overwhelming magic of the imagination.

They would turn the corner into the living room, stop cold, eyes large, stare, mouths open. Then they started to jump up and down, squeaking like frightened mice. Lord, have mercy, how do you handle that? Sleepy lumps of human joy unfettered by war, by depression, by fear, by knowledge, even? They had only the vaguest notion of their parents' lives and scarcely time or space to store such information.

I never dwelled on it, but I suspected Bayer and Greta had conversations about me and the holidays and all that. They knew my story. I'm sure they thought I was hanging around, trying to piggyback some of the childhood I didn't have. You know what? I don't want to talk about it.

Right now, I had my weary arms full. If Robin hadn't been in her wheelchair, I don't think I would have recognized her. I had never seen her at eye level. She had always been three or four feet above me on her porch. She seemed pudgier than I remembered. It could be her winter clothes, or the years since I'd seen her.

"What are you doing here?"

"Aren't ya glad to see me, Yank?"

"Glad is too vague. Where's Octane?"

"Octavio."

"Octavio."

"He's back in Georgia."

"Why aren't you with him?"

"He's dead. I buried him there, after his accident at the Ford plant in Detroit."

"I'm really sorry."

"He was a Democrat."

"Tell me you're not part of Nine Mile."

"I'm not part of Nine Mile."

"You *are* part of Nine Mile, or you wouldn't have known what I meant."

"I'm not. I'm not. But they are paying me a small bundle to get close to you."

"Octavio is out in the car, isn't he?"

"No, he really is in Georgia."

"And dead?"

"I hope so. I had him cremated."

"What about the fake mother?"

"Octavio's mother? She's real, let me tell you."

"No, the woman in the black fur coat. She went out just as you came in."

"Oh, you spotted her."

"I did."

"She's not a fake mother. She's the boss."

"The boss?"

"The big banana."

"I know what boss . . . you mean the head of Nine Mile? A lady?"

"She's got it in for you. She said she built an honest business after the war, and you made her burn it down and start over."

"You're a bit forthcoming for someone on her payroll."

"Well, it's like this. I'm not on her payroll. I work per diem. Something for something."

"Forsooth."

"I'm not sure what that means."

"It means unlock your wheelchair and follow me. Better yet, you get in front of me, where I can keep an eye on you."

"You're not afraid of a girl, are you?"

Chapter Thirty

"I'm uncomfortable."
"How so?
"I'm anxious."
"Just because an organized crime outfit has your number?"
"Yes."

***

As Robin and I wheeled past Bayer, heading for the warehouse, I told him I was heading out to make the Christmas Eve deliveries for the customer who wanted their kids in bed before their presents showed up.

"This is Robin, from Mt. Clemens. She's going to ride along with me."

Bayer gave me his folded forehead look. But it was closing time on Christmas Eve, and he had other things to think about. I guided Robin through the Store to the unheated warehouse, where we parked the old Ford pickup in winter. Robin craned her head around.

"Is this where you dismember people like me?"

"We do. But not on Christmas Eve."

I opened the big door and hit the buzzer to remind Bayer to come and close it after I pulled out. Then, with a lot of tugging and harrumphing, we climbed in and pulled our disassembled and telescope folded wheelchairs in after us. We couldn't see each other with the four wheels and flattened chairs between us—much of it on her lap—but we could talk.

"Just how do you propose to 'get close to me' for this Nine Mile money you're making?"

"The usual way."

I tried to give her a sidelong ironic look, but when I turned my face, I got a mouthful of wheelchair tire. We drove through town toward the river, past shops and street lamps hung with oversized wreaths. Plow trucks were still clearing snowbanks, days after the big snow.

"Her first plan was to bring the store down on a morals charge, but you never took the bait."

"A what charge?"

"You were supposed to try to get into Skyler's pants."

"What!"

"Skyler is the boss's daughter. You were supposed to try something untoward."

"You're starting to make me nervous."

"How come you never laid a hand on her? Did the Japs shoot it off?"

"I don't believe that. Unbelievable."

"When nothing happened, the boss got her a teaching job somewhere out in missed-a-belt-loop Arkansas."

"Missouri."

"Missouri."

"I don't believe you guys. This is nuts."

"It's not me, Yank. I'm an innocent vendor . . . consultant . . . migrant laborer, whatever you want to call me. So, what was the hang up with Skyler?

"Skyler's not that kind of girl."

"Woman."

"She wore long jean skirts that covered her ankles, and puffy white blouses. Those are signs. Guys pick up on that."

"Not in West Tennessee."

"It's like when you go to a dance. First thing a guy does is check out the shoes. If you see a girl wearing shoes that are hard to dance in, you know she's not there to dance."

"Yeah, well, Mr. Man-of-the-World, doesn't . . ."

"Doesn't work like that in West Tennessee because everybody's barefoot."

We drove in silence for a bit. The Skyler thing really threw me. I think I started shivering a little, and not from the chill of winter. The gifts in the back belonged to a doctor who lived in a townhouse near the river bridge, just across the street from the big white UCC church, Reverend Watkins' church no less.

I tooted the horn two short burps, trying not to wake up their kids. Their nanny came right out and unloaded the truck, thank you very much.

"What's going on in that church? All the lights are on, and people are going in?"

"Some kind of Christmas Eve service."

"Let's go. I've never been to one. Come on. It's Christmas Eve after all."

"Hence . . ."

"Have I ever asked for anything before?"

"Don't make me laugh. I'll have to take a leak. We're not dressed for church."

"We've got shoes on, which is all you need in . . .

"West Tennessee."

Chapter Thirty-One

What do you mean it all catches up with you—eventually?
It's the conscience.
Not my conscience.
Can't escape it.
I've always been semi-conscious.
For you, that's not a bad answer.

***

It's damn hard to walk into church when you haven't been there since you were baptized. And coming in in a wheelchair just adds to it. Watkins had a crude ramp built, the only church in town that had one. The war hero had said he wanted to find a place for those guys chewed up by the war. Smooth talker, Watkins.

It jars the senses: coming from the dark and the cold into a vaulted, over-lit sanctuary, buzzing with men in baggy suits and women in hats and bits of fox fur. Right away, Deacons and Deacon apprentices—or whatever they are called—hurried to help us. Against my polite wishes, they tugged us out of our chairs and plopped us on a purple, tufted pew cushion. At least we were in the last pew and off to the side. Someone then rolled our chairs out of sight in a back hallway. I found that unnerving and was thinking of telling him we didn't come for the service; we just came in to ask directions.

Watkins, in a white pulpit gown and purple stole, came royally down the aisle to lay hands on the infirm.

"Lieutenant Watkins, I'm Captain Zadoc. Been a while."

The Reverend's holiday cheer curdled a bit.

"This is Robin, of West Tennessee."

The war hero gave me a two-finger handshake but took Robin's hand in his two and welcomed her to "our little church." Then he walked swiftly back to the pulpit, indicating to the nearly full house that it was time to start the service. Robin leaned on my shoulder.

"When they take my chair away, it makes me feel like I have to pee."

"I have that same feeling."

On cue, the house lights dimmed a bit, and Watkins began.

"We are gathered here tonight, Lord, called by the promise of your Presence here with us this Christmas Eve. See into our hearts, read the love that is written there. Accept our sorrow for our faults and omissions . . ."

At that moment, the hips of a middle-aged woman in a black fur coat screwdrivered into the narrow slot between me and the pew arm rest, squeezing me tight against Robin. I started to tell her there was plenty of space on the other side of Robin. I pulled my head up and a little away to see her, and even before I got a good look, it clicked.

"What have we here?" I said to myself. "The little lady running Nine Mile?"

Then Robin leaned forward, got a look, and clapped a hand over her mouth. I turned back to the hips: it was the fake mother. The boss? Shit Mother. For a quick second, I wondered if the guys who took our wheelchairs were in on this.

I snapped back toward Robin. She was giving me the large eyeball, "I had nothing to do with this" look. My pulse went way up and started thumping. But what is this? What is happening? Instinctively, I kept my arm cocked, ready to fend off a knife or a gun. But something about her calmness—she was listening to Watkins drone on—made me feel that this kind of thing wasn't in the cards. She had plenty of hired hands for the hard stuff. Even so, nothing here made sense. I had to move.

If this was just to unnerve me, it was succeeding. The kicker was Robin. She was struggling to breathe, and that affected my breathing. So much unnatural breathing going on here, so two elderly ladies in front of us turned around and gave us one of those turn-of-the-century snort looks.

Gingerly, I turned my head back to the Big Banana. No acknowledgement of my glance, even with our hips and arms butting. I couldn't see her eyes. She had one of those 1920s clochey things that covered her face from the side. All I could see was a strong chin and the tip of an ordinary Midwest, Indo-European, Northern Caucasian nose. (Truth: I hadn't the slightest idea of what kind of nose she had.)

"Would you like a bulletin?"

Nothing. A determined and quite successful will, to be squashed against me and not acknowledge my presence. This could mean one of three things. Then I couldn't think of what the three things were. I was unraveling.

I can't unravel, I'm a combat veteran. But I'm a combat veteran with three minutes of combat brought low before the first Jap popped up.

I shot my right arm straight up in the air and waved at Watkins.

We are here this Christmas Eve to celebrate the promise of our Lord Christ's birth and our own renewal . . .

"Yes?"

"I would like to present the message tonight, Reverend."

I turned my head toward the center of the room.

"Reverend Watkins saved my life during the war, and I promised him I would repay him someday by presenting the sermon in his church."

Someone in the congregation said, "That's beautiful," and others began to clap, in a modest, churchy way. Watkins was smart enough to realize he'd lost control of the service.

They brought up my wheelchair, and "Mrs. B" stood up silently to give me room to transfer. I glanced at Robin. She gave me the raised eyebrow "smart move" look.

Watkins gave an awkward introduction about the special bonds of men at war, probably something he had read, and I started in on a spiel I'd been prepping for my next religious tug of war with Farmer Gordon.

"I think it's only natural on this Christmas Eve that we think about the two commandments Jesus said were the most important . . ."

Bayer, Greta, and their oldest, Elizabeth, are sitting right in front of me in the first row! Bayer has that bemused "What the hell are you doing?" look. Greta has her German scowl on, and Elizabeth is smiling through her braces. I went back to the book of Matthew, but my mind was racing to figure out how to tell Bayer what was going on.

" 'You shall love the Lord your God with all your heart, and with all your soul, and with all your mind.' This is the greatest and first commandment. And a second is like it: 'You shall love your neighbor as yourself.' Does that mean we should walk a mile in our neighbor's shoes, or perhaps nine miles in our neighbor's shoes. Think about that, a *nine-mile* walk."

I looked straight at Bayer, and tried, with my head and eyes, to indicate that he needed to check out the back row.

"Nine miles is a long way to walk, even in your own shoes, much less your neighbor's shoes . . ."

Bayer has his brow furled but hasn't gotten the message.

" 'Do unto others as you would have others do unto you.' Matthew 7:12. All four Gospels report this; all his actions showed us how this is done, right up to dying for us that we might have Eternal Life. He tried to make things easy for us, reducing all the Law to one short phrase: 'Do as you would have done for you.' It's so simple! If you would wish to have enough food, feed the hungry. If you would wish to have shelter, provide a home. If you would have peace, make peace; walk the nine miles. Think of getting up and walking up the aisle tonight as the beginning of a nine-mile journey . . ."

Bayer—finally—gets up and heads up the aisle toward the back.

"Okay, ladies and gentlemen, let's turn off the lights now, light our candles and sing Silent Night."

I heard Watkins start to object, as there was more to the service, but the lights went right out, and the organist began. Sharp staff at this church. I followed Bayer up the aisle in the dark.

Chapter Thirty-Two

Ignore it.
How can I ignore something that won't ignore me?
Well then, just pretend to ignore it.
That's the best you've got?
Ignorance is often essential.
Many people don't know that.

***

I never read crime novels. Can't stand gratuitous pain as entertainment. And to be in one in real life upsets the soul. Makes you wonder if life in general plays out like some low-grade crime. The elderly seem to know the answer to that but they don't want to talk about it.

I found Bayer on the sidewalk, standing in the dull light of two globes lighting the granite steps of the church. It was beginning to snow in spurts. A shark-finned Lincoln Continental had stopped in the street, and the B lady was standing in front of its huge passenger door, held open for her by one of her raincoated rum runners.

She's standing still, staring at Bayer.

I wheeled up beside him.

"What are we looking at, the wife of the Nine Mile guy?"

"She is the Nine Mile guy."

"Seriously."

"She's the little sweetheart that got you canned in Pittsburgh."

"Why is she here? She was in church."

I decided to break this silent stand-off.

"Why are you here?"

The B lady didn't move a muscle, just stood there, calmly looking at us even as the occasional car had to go around her big Continental. Robin pulled up beside us. We could faintly hear the congregation singing Silent Night.

I looked up at Bayer,

"What do you think we should do?"

"Go back and get our coats."

"And?"

"Go home."

Before we turned away, the B Lady climbed silently into the car, followed by her goon, and the thick door closed with a wump. The big car glided away.

I asked Bayer, "Think she'll try something while's she's in town?"

"I don't think so, she wouldn't have shown herself. How did you know who she was?"

We started making our way back to the church.

"Robin here, your former neighbor in Mt. Clemens, works for her."

We all stopped.

"Used to work for her, I mean. Her husband died and she needed some money. We're getting married."

Bayer looked at both of us. Robin looked at me. Bayer wouldn't say so, but I'm sure he was thinking this was rather sudden.

"We've been thinking about it for several years."

"Even before Octavio died," Robin said.

Then, she looked up at Bayer.

"He was a New Deal Democrat."

Bayer smiled. (Go Robin!)

"What's that noise?" he said.

I could still hear Silent Night coming from inside, but there was another noise, the gurgling sound of running water. In the snow-covered bushes near the steps, someone had opened the church's outdoor faucet. The water was cutting a channel through the snow as it made its way to the sidewalk. Bayer stepped into the snow and turned it off.

"What the hell is that all about?" he said.

I looked back to see if the Continental had returned. The street was quiet.

"I think she's just raining on our parade," Robin said. "Criminals are never happy, 'specially on Christmas Eve."

Words like that sound philosophical on a cold night when you're ready to claw into a snowbank and sleep. I drove Robin to the only hotel in town, retrieved her bags, six of them, parked the truck in the warehouse and took Fretty up to my little apartment.

Robin looked it over.

"Livin' large, hey Yank?"

"Wait till you see the bed."

"Where's the bedroom?"

"You're standing in it."

"When are we getting married?"

"In about five minutes."

The wedding proved chaste. By the time we got our shoes off and transferred to my couch bed and pulled a wool blanket over us, we were sound asleep—and rather content.

Chapter Thirty-Three

Running water is a sign.
Of what?
A leak somewhere.
In what?
In your thinking, perhaps.
I think you have a leak somewhere.

***

We woke up during that first night and kissed for the first time.

"Is that your real name, Robin?"

"T'is."

"And what's your last name? I don't think you ever told me."

"Ravenal. Of the Tennessee Ravenals."

"Your married name or your maiden name?"

"My stage name."

"Really. And what stage are you going through right now?"

We tried, half-heartedly, to fool around, but we were far too spent—not to mention that we were getting reacquainted after having been not so acquainted in the first place. Not that we didn't know. We knew. We had known since the beginning.

Beyond that, we had the same model wheelchair. Small thing, but there it is. And now we had Nine Mile in common. So, there was that. And, somewhat obliquely, I was indirectly responsible for almost killing her, having given that wood-splitting maul to Octavio. I have no evidence, but I'm sure some great marriages have been built on less.

And we did get married, both in bed and in the eyes of God. Watkins stood in for God, and we had a small but cheerful luncheon at the Lewisburger Hotel with the Watkins, Greta and Bayer and their three older children.

Don't get me wrong, we had great sex. Just not the kind of sex you have, or had, or thought about having. When four legs do not function, there is still much to be done that borders on the outer limits of solid geometry—including the mysteries of mathematical symmetry and three-dimensional probability. What struck me was her feminine self. We transferred from our wheelchairs to the couch or to the toilet the exact same way. But when she moved about, there was a difference—her gentle womanly form. It captivated me and made my face feel warm. Even though I conked out within five seconds of closing my eyes that first night, I fell in love with her before sleep came.

We lasted about ten days in my pinthouse. Our lifeless legs just couldn't take the battering anymore—metal on bones. So, we scrambled into the first floor of an old, wood-framed, two-story rental, right behind the Store. Now we had a real bedroom, a kitchen roomy enough for two, a kind of dining-room living-room, and a front room on the street that was probably meant to be a small formal parlor. The front door led to three steps down to the sidewalk, so we used the back door, which was level with a little parking area. The parlor gradually became a kind of storage-junk room.

We called our new house Warehouse Number Two, and eventually "The Warehouse." It was so much larger than the pinthouse. I found it depressing at first, with the empty rooms and the old paint. Robin spent a busy month getting rid of my old stuff, installing curtains, buying copies of Persian rugs and some sturdy colonial-type furniture, and adding what she called accent pieces. With her changes, the place came alive and felt inviting and comfortable. That was an eye-opener for me.

115

A few months later, she and Bayer came up with idea of building a "Kitchen of the Future" toward the back of the Store. Robin would run it and draw a commission on her sales. The town already had a good appliance store, selling major brands like Westinghouse and Amana. Robin's kitchen, while not as pricey, was a real working kitchen with running water and working ovens. Every day, she made bread or cookies. The novelty and the aroma attracted a steady stream of women—and made serious money. A lot of the women were enchanted with her West Tennessee accent.

"Is that woman from Texas?"

"Tennessee."

"I knew it had to be Texas or Tennessee."

Even the Reverend, who either had an appetite for still warm chocolate chip cookies—or a certain fascination for Robin—came by regularly, now that he realized we weren't going to shoot him for lying about his war record. The only one not enchanted with her accent, the aroma of fresh bread, and the Kitchen of the Future, was the elder Bayer, who once again had to move his big oak desk to make room for all the changes.

"Well, for cryin' out loud."

One day, at age 92, he worked (and slept) his usual stint at the Store, then went around and said goodnight to me and Bayer—something he never did—and drove home and died.

He had never recovered from his professional peak at age 58 in 1933. His world had shrunk to naught—a word from his time. The two or three men who occasionally stopped by the Store to chat with him, men who also came of age in the 1800s, had died off twenty years earlier.

That spring, I think it was early March, I wheeled around to the front steps of our rental. I wanted to see if there was an easy way to ramp the front door. We could save a lot of chugging if we could come and go from the front door. The snow was still piled high next to the curb and along the front of the house. But the sun was warm, and everything was melting fast. While sitting there, I heard rushing water. Not street run-off—real rushing water like rapids in a stream.

I got it. The Christmas Eve omen. I had never seen it, but Bayer had told me years ago there was a stream running right under the buildings across the street. With warm weather coming on and record-making snow piled up all over town, it sounded like that stream was going to flood.

I went back to the Store to find Bayer.

"We need five hundred sandbags, and we need them tomorrow."

"You think so?"

"I know so."

We found only two hundred sandbags, and it took three days to get them, and most of an afternoon for our beleaguered Bobby Spring, our snow guy, to pile them around the Store's basement windows and coal chute. By the time he finished, the water was already a couple inches deep on the sidewalk.

At least we might save the big boiler by keeping most of the water out of the basement. The Store sat more than three feet above the sidewalk on the water side. If it got higher than that, we were in big trouble.

For the next several days, as the sun climbed higher, the daily melt-off swirled down the sidewalk. To our relief, it never got more than three or four inches deep. The sandbags held. The hidden stream did not overflow. And the school kids on their way home in the afternoon had fun splashing in the water.

Crisis over.

Bayer and I kept an eye on things from the side windows overlooking the street.

"Do you think that's what the Christmas Eve thing was all about?"

I wasn't sure.

"I don't know. We're in a low part of town, and that stream isn't going away."

Chapter Thirty-Four

Did you sweep the floor?
I swept the floor.
Did you vacuum the toy section?
I vacuumed the toy section.
Did you re-order everything we sold in auto parts?
I re-ordered everything we sold in auto parts.
Good.

***

No one needs to explain ordinary. We know ordinary. We do ordinary. We just don't think about it or talk about it. Ordinary is not celebrated until it goes missing.

For Bayer, Robin, and me, the next eight years were ordinary. Six mornings a week, at eight thirty in the morning, I rolled up the sidewalk to the front of the Store, unlocked the door and pulled the strings—with some stretching—on twenty-four overhead fluorescent lights. I opened the cabinet-size safe, put the cash drawer back in the cash register, and got a pot of coffee percolating on a two-burner on the shelf behind Bayer's desk.

When Bayer came in, generally a few minutes after me, we'd have coffee and chat about the day's work. How were we going to set up for fishing season, for hunting season? Who was waiting anxiously for a car part that didn't show up on the regular Thursday delivery truck? Anything on back order meant waiting another week.

The pleasant hum of ordinary went deeper than that. On a slow summer afternoon, I might spend an hour or so in the cool warehouse, sorting through stands of curiously bent exhaust and tail pipes and stacks of mufflers. Did we have one each on hand for the most popular year and models of Fords, Chevrolets, Pontiacs, Plymouths, and Dodges? Or, on a snowy winter day, with the steam radiators softly whistling, I might take an hour to sift through the big drawers of windshield wipers. Here, we kept one in inventory for every type of car and truck our regulars drove, including Ramblers, Studebakers, and even some old DeSotos.

Over the years, Bayer's children showed up for work intermittently as they made their way through junior and senior high school. The oldest, Elizabeth, emulated her father: quiet, diligent, concerned about the customers.

"Dad, this woman needs a new tire right away. She has to drive a hundred and twenty miles today to bring her mother home to live with them."

She became a schoolteacher, wife, and mother of two.

The boy, Chase, delivered sales flyers to every house in our town of five thousand. In the Store, he was shy with customers and spent most of his time in the warehouse—repairing, sometimes destroying, used lawnmowers and outboard boat motors that customers traded in for new models. He got a degree in engineering, went into the Army, and eventually became a business writer.

Margot, the next in line, showed up, put her hands on her hips and declared that the Store needed an overhaul.

"I think we'll start with a bicycle parts section right here."

Over time, she took a shine to a kid working as a soda jerk at the drug store uptown. She began disappearing for hours at a time. To cover her tracks, she would issue orders to me and Bayer, things she wanted done while she "ran a few errands."

"I need eighteen boxes this size, twelve that size, and six like this one. I'll also need printable labels for each."

One day, her "to do" list for us was so long we feared she and the kid might be headed to Mexico to elope.

She eventually married the soda jerk. He became a doctor, she a college professor, and they raised four children.

I don't remember much about the youngest one, Zuzie. She came along five years after Margot. She spent some time at the Store, working with Robin, and went on to teach school and raise two children.

I vividly recall how Bayer handled each of them. It was just like being back on his ship in the Pacific. He set the tone by his sober example and let each youngster tackle the chores of ordinary by the light of whichever star or planet they came from. It reminded me of Heinz and Vinnie and Hennessey and the rest of his crew going about the work of war, doing what needed to be done without waiting for someone to bark at them. Minus Watkins, of course.

It takes a certain genius to do this, said old Clausewitz. I don't mean to overstate this but from what I watched, it struck me how parenting paralleled war. As per custom, the adult operates with only a foggy notion of the kids' actions. Yet, the commander with a genius for war manages to see the big picture—through the fog—and make the right strategic decisions.

Is this intuitive or learned? Who knows?

Bayer never said much about what happened in '33 when the banks closed, and he went from the tennis courts at Albion to the streets of Detroit. For me, it was like going home. For him, it had to have been a preview of the apocalypse. But I'm guessing that instead of caving, like his dad, he had an epiphany.

"Is this the worst there is?"

Like General Grant in the Civil War, when he realized the rebels were as afraid of him as he was of them, he calmed down and began winning battles. That was Bayer's hallmark in war and kid-raising: calm.

However, victories may be earned, they're a badge not easily won. Or so it seems to me.

In an unspoken and perhaps undetectable way, we both luxuriated in this predictable world of ordinary life. We were primed. The Depression and the war had scared us. Life can turn bad quickly. It's a notion obvious to anyone, but to those who lived it, smelled the blood, tasted the tears, and ran dry on hope, ordinary—the mundane—is a happy miracle.

More than half our customers, it seemed, were veterans. A few of them had been ground up and deformed for life. All of them, though, even the ones who had an "easy" war, found their natural focus altered. They tended to look out and away now and then when talking, not the thousand-yard stare of the combat haunted, necessarily, more the way a frustrated teacher does in front of oblivious students. Two or three of them never got over the fright. When they were in the Store, they stood flat-footed, heavy, and blinked non-stop. They didn't prosper.

We were content with this ordinary life for as long as it lasted because we knew it wouldn't last forever. We'd been happily pecking away at this for more than twenty years by now, and we weren't kids when we started. Bayer and I were beginning to look a little careworn, as was the Store. Except for their youngest, Bayer and Greta had translated tires, lawnmowers, fishing rods, and shotgun shells into college educations for their brood.

Robin did so well perfuming the store, and possibly the whole block, with the aroma of baking breads and cookies, she essentially ran an unlicensed café at the back of the Store. A regular crowd, often including Watkins and Farmer Gordon, came for the coffee and her southern style sticky buns, but also to marvel that a woman in a wheelchair could actually do things. They also loved her accent and arch Southerness.

"You Yanks don't know corn bread from boiled peanuts."

Change comes with clouds. And one cloud on the horizon was a new type of retail, called a shopping mall. Two of these malls had opened in nearby cities, and we saw our business beginning to thin out a bit. We weren't terribly worried because we had an upper hand—we were local, and people knew us by our names.

Then a big black cloud dropped right out of the sky. I was talking with Bedford, the assistant manager at the bank.

"You didn't hear that the new building uptown is going to be a hardware store?"

"No, I didn't."

"Well, that's a little odd. Your wife is their local representative—some out of state outfit."

"My wife!"

"It's not such a big deal. She just has power of attorney to sign local papers in their absence. Anybody in town could do it."

By the time I got back to the Store, it was raining heavily. Real rain.

Chapter Thirty-Five

I told you from the beginning.

We've been married for eight years. Eight years.

I'm aware of that.

What is this? Is it the Civil War? Tennessee was on our side, you know.

East *Tennessee was on your side.*

I don't believe this.

Yeah, well, kiss my ass, you carpet-bagging blue belly.

Yeah, well, you can kiss this marriage good-bye.

Suits me fine, you Lincoln-loving loser.

***

My "discussion" with Robin that night isn't printable here. (I'm writing this in a small village in the lumbering woods of Maine, and there are children about.)

The thunderstorm outside grew into a dark blanket of water. Streetlights came on at mid-afternoon. I didn't go back to the Store. I went straight home. The storm inside our first floor monoplex seemed even darker, with flashes of lightning coming in shrill epithets.

I hounded Robin from the back door to the dining room and back again—our wheelchairs clanking off each other, cries of "ouch" and "watch it" as our feet and arms collided with furniture and walls.

This was cold-blooded treason, and I was complicit. I married a woman who told me straight up she worked for Nine Mile. I was livid with myself for thinking it was a joke. My strange power to see things coming, at least a few things, did not include anything touched by Nine Mile.

That was pretty clear now, and it chilled me to the bone. I took it out on Robin. The things I yelled at her in those dark hours broke the bonds of attachment and likely weakened the Enlightenment's notion of what it means to be human.

I might as well have been standing on a mountain, screaming at Original Sin.

Except we weren't on a mountain top. We were in the lowest part of town, across the street from an unseen stream bed, and rain had been cascading at more than two inches an hour for hours. On our last war lap around the kitchen, the tires on our wheelchairs started throwing up a spray of water. Runoff, tumbling down the gentle slope from the parking lot outside, was streaming under the kitchen door. I opened it to see how it was out there. Mistake. The door had been holding back a dam of two or three inches of water.

I slammed the door shut as the water rolled all the way through the house to the front door. I stuffed kitchen towels against the door, but it only slowed the seepage. I wheeled to the front door. I wanted to see how the street looked. Our rugs were soaked through and squishy. It took me a few minutes to plow through the bookcases and suitcases and stuff that we had piled up in the parlor.

When I got the front door open, it took me a minute to understand what I was looking at. I heard Robin sobbing and talking on the phone.

"Come and get me, Tom. Zadoc has lost his mind."

Tom? She's calling Watkins?

The street looked normal enough, until it got through to me that I wasn't looking at the street. What the hell? The streetlights had gone out. My mind saw the street, but the street wasn't there. As my eyes adjusted to the dark, the depth of trouble we were in came clear. Water was rolling over the top step to our front door. The hidden stream had come out from its hiding place. The street was three feet under water. I could feel it rising in the short time I was sitting there.

Damn, too late to call Bobby Spring to bring the sandbags up from the Store basement. The boiler must be under water by now.

My stomach started to feel weightless and unhappy.

I yelled to Robin who was still on the kitchen phone:

"Better tell old Tom to bring a boat."

Time to change gears. War with Robin would have to wait for a sunnier day. We were surrounded. Time to get a breakout plan and make it work.

"Call Bayer at home. Tell him the street's flooding. Bring the truck we need to get out of here."

"Can't."

"Why not?"

"Phone just died."

"Shit."

I wheeled through what now felt like three inches of water in the house and tried to open the back door. Swollen shut. I tried prying it with kitchen knives and a screwdriver. Nothing. I wheeled back to the street door and got it open just as water started flowing into the house from the street.

If we tried to get out now, our wheelchairs would capsize in the current, and we would be flotsam. It had been a muggy July day when this started, but this flood water felt cold, now soaking through my shoes and splashing up to my knees as I moved around.

I looked at Robin in the kitchen light. She was still sobbing. I couldn't tell if she was cold. An empty suitcase started floating across the floor. Then the lights went out.

Our only way out now was the front door, and only if someone showed up with a boat. I had heard of flood waters rising incredibly fast, but nothing like this. Of course, we had been lost in our battle of regrets and recriminations for hours. The water inside was over a foot deep now and making different sounds as it got deeper. I could hear more things moving about, bumping, and quietly rubbing against the walls.

"Robin, come over here. We have to sit on the stairway. If the current comes back on, we'll get a shock."

The house's original staircase, before it was divided into apartments, was still there, leading to a false ceiling. Only thing I could think of was to sit our fannies on the steps and keep bumping up higher as the water rose. If it got all the way to the ceiling, I would try to break the plaster with my hands. After that, I had no idea. If there was a solid plywood floor above the plaster, that's where we would drown.

I had a hard time getting Robin to let go of her wheelchair and transfer to the stairs. The chair is our lifeline, our legs, our only source of freedom. Off the wheelchair, we don't feel natural or even comfortable.

She felt the water climbing up her legs, so—finally—she let me pull her out and rudely plop her on the stairs. We sat side by side without talking. After what seemed like just a few minutes, we had to bump up a stair to stay out of the water.

The rain started up again, in solid sheets. A minute later we heard a loud thunk at the back door, followed by banging and shouting. Watkins!

"The front door! Come around to the street door!"

We shouted as loud as we could. It took the Great Navigator another 30 minutes till the bow of his tiny aluminum fishing boat poked through the door. We couldn't see him, but his flashlight beam darted about the parlor, now a good two feet under water.

I pushed off the stairs into the water and grabbed the bow of his boat. The current kicking up in the street was trying to pull it out. I braced against the front wall, and with my other arm, grabbed Robin's arm, pulled her off the steps and into the water. She grabbed the gunnel with both hands, and I pushed and pulled her up by the fanny and dumped her headfirst into the tiny boat. She righted herself, like a mad cat, and grabbed my face with both hands.

"You come, too!"

"Can't. I know this boat. Too small. It's made for one person."

She held my face tight, fingers spread, nails digging into me. Her eyes swollen, her nose running, in the flashlight beam I wouldn't have known her.

"I love you, Yank."

She let go of my face. I let go of the boat. It catapulted into the current.

"I love you, too."

I shouted to Watkins.

"Stay away from the other side of the street! Turn up the next side street, away from the stream over there!"

I turned back to the staircase.

They didn't make it to the next side street. One of Watkins' oars probably hit some debris and jumped out of its oarlock. They were pulled to the other side of the street and quickly swept between two buildings situated right over the old stream bed. There they broached in a standing wave against the downstream building. The little boat soon flipped, and they were dragged under the building. Both got trapped in debris under there and quickly drowned.

Chapter Thirty-Six

What the hell?

Sorry?

When I say what the hell, it's a question, not a statement.

I believe you.

Well?

Well, what?

***

Later that night, our police chief, Gordie, tried to save someone further down the street. His boat overturned and he drowned. They called off rescue attempts after that, and I spent most of the night scooting backward up the stairs.

Bayer somehow got his homebuilt outboard through the do-not-cross lines and docked behind our house. I shouted to him, and in about twenty minutes he chopped a hole through the floor over my head. Scary as hell, but it worked. The young Bucknell student couple who lived above us were gone for the summer. They never returned.

The next dreary hot month was the worst of my life, worse than reform school, getting thrown out of Albion, prison, and the war—combined. We buried Robin and Watkins. One of the firefighters told me we were lucky to have their bodies. Everything silts over in floods, and bodies are hard to find after that. Fortunately, both weren't far from where the little boat capsized. At their combined funeral, I started to realize I'd been wrong about Watkins.

I'm not a get-up-say-my-prayers-go-to-work-come-home-read-the-Bible-go-to-bed guy. Watkins was. He had played football at Notre

Dame, but he wasn't a football guy. He wasn't even Catholic. And he should have never been at sea as a line officer. From the bits I heard from friends and family at the service, he never had any ambition beyond slinging the Gospel and shepherding a congregation. He risked his life trying to pull Robin away from me and the flood.

Odd, sometimes, how we see people differently when they are freshly dead.

Robin, on the other hand, remained a painful, goddamned mystery. I was so ripped up between anger and loss, I fell into one of those freshman psych things—a double approach-avoidance complex. (I took it seriously, my time at Albion.) When I thought about her, I got angry. Did she somehow cause this flood? When I didn't think about her, I missed her.

Too bad Watkins was dead. At the funeral, everyone looked to me to say something about her. I think Watkins knew more about her than I did. For the last several years, they seemed to have long conversations over coffee in Robin's display kitchen in the Store. Odd, how two can live together for eight years and not really know much about each other.

Her drowning and the night of sitting there waiting my turn to drown gutted something in my brain. New and strange thoughts rose up—a certain and painful intellectual inadequacy. My mind repeatedly tried to float away, as though none of this had happened. But I kept crawling back to reality, albeit feebly.

There was the disagreeable stuff. Five feet of sticky, silted, filthy flood water ruined the Store's inventory, buckled the floor, soaked the walls, and made a mess of the displays. The building would have to be gutted. That meant gutting Bayer's retirement, too. No one had flood insurance in those days. Worse, just cleaning up, much less replacing the heating, wiring, floors, and walls, would mean going into debt. At the funeral and reception, everyone asked Bayer about the Store. He told them the only thing he could say.

"We'll see."

The morning following the funeral, we saw the Store. Bayer and I and some white-haired factotum from the county health department had just made a sticky, sloshy walk-through and were back out on the sidewalk in front of it. I had the feeling I'd just wheeled through the innards of a large dead animal. Bayer and the county guy were talking quietly. My mind started to drift.

Badly manhandled by Mother Nature, it started asking absurd questions and expected answers. If I had sat on a mountain top for years, would I have figured out that the Earth revolves around the sun? No. If I had happened upon a vein of iron ore, would I have developed steel? No. Would I have invented the wheel? No. Discovered oxygen and nitrogen? Wheedled the mysteries of geometry from a simple triangle? No. Developed a simple algebra formula? Never. Invented weaving, farming, how to splice an apple tree? Developed a code of morality, conjured a religion, organized a community, led a tribe?

Everything I knew was secondhand knowledge.

I was fifty-something-years-old and had never had an original thought. Everything in my brain, body, and soul was someone else's invention.

I remembered the old fuddster in English at Albion, saying that T. S. Eliot, of whom I knew zilch, said it was hard to figure out what is really new. Worse, I had no idea what any of these thoughts had to do with the flood and Robin and Watkins. But I felt my vision starting to go dark, as though some tiny person in my head was squeezing my eyeballs. I know some people call this disassociation, or something like that—a trauma-induced whatever. But I call it squeezed eyeballs going dark.

Everything looks a tad grim from a wheelchair. This wasn't that. My lights were going out, even as I listened to Bayer and this guy talking about sewage and health hazards, their voices now muted and distant.

It may have been a delayed shock reaction—what do I know?

My brain continued tracking on its own. In this early morning eclipse, it continued to attack me. After a lifetime of observation, what could I say about the human condition? What? Nothing. Leave me alone. You don't get what's at stake here, do you? No. We want to know if your life was worth anything. "Who's we?" Never mind that, it's just the grammar of convenience. We think you have been sleepwalking through life.

That struck home. It made me start to think. I had been—what to call it—detached. My eight years with Robin seemed a quiet murmur, broken by an occasional laugh or angry word. Is that possible? Eight years reduced to vague background noise? It felt like I had been more awake with Skyler, and we never got involved, or even in bed. And twenty-five years with the Store—twenty-six! Nothing, almost a blank. Even the war, and my legs, not small potatoes, felt muted. Isn't this natural? Isn't everyone . . . or was there some point where I stopped being here full-time and started shutting down? The fire that killed my family, reform school, prison? You know the answer, you piker, quit stalling.

It was that night at the fraternity house. I was the big cheese in charge of hazing the pledges. I was full of myself—from wretched orphan and small-time crook to Master of the Realm at the TKE house. Then, I kicked this rich kid from Detroit in the back and slipped off my little perch.

You can't tell this tepid story to an otherwise thoughtful bystander. An autumn leaf would seem to carry more weight. But there it is—the turning point. I see it clearly. I am awake again. Can I have my eyesight and my hearing back?

My temperature spiked, very fast, and as sweat streamed off my face and soaked through my shirt and trousers, my arms sagged, my back bent, and my head flopped forward. But my hearing started to come back, and then, slowly, my eyesight. I was still sitting in my wheelchair on the hot sidewalk in front of the Store, soaking wet, collapsed, but back with the living.

I heard the health officer saying, "What's the matter with him?"

I gave him an "up yours" glance.

"Touch of Jap malaria."

"Is it contagious?"

Chapter Thirty-Seven

What's all this?
Just me.
You've changed.
I like to think I've evolved.
Since last week?

***

The disaster that killed Robin and Watkins and wiped out the Store killed a bunch of people in Pennsylvania that summer and destroyed 3,000 businesses. Some kind of hurricane rains came way inland. It also stirred up an odd assortment of humans.

The better people showed up first. Amish men, in groups of three and four, quietly walked into the Store and began scooping up buckets of silt and debris. They talked little and worked non-stop for hours—men who seemed to be all muscle and smiles as they labored. I watched them in awe. They were customers, but we didn't know them well, as they rarely indulged in chit-chat.

Next, came a ragged parade of grifters and jackals, eager to make a buck off the backside of disaster. First up was a hoary faced fat tub from New Jersey in a rented truck. After a quick walk-through, and nary sign of any inner humanity, he announced he would buy all of our tires, exhaust pipes, and mufflers for pennies on the dollar. He knew very well that the law would not allow us to sell any of our flood-stained inventory at retail.

Bayer chatted with him for a few minutes and got him to double his offer. He then produced two surprisingly normal-looking sons who set about collecting the parts. Something about their efficient eagerness tripped my internal alarm. I spoke up, loudly.

"Nothing, and I mean nothing, goes on the truck till cash changes hands. No checks, cash. And for the agreed amount. Just stop what you're doing, gentlemen."

Bayer stared at me.

"Oldest trick in the book. Stuff the truck, then come back and offer a pittance, and then leave it up to us to unload the truck and put everything back."

Before Bayer could argue for the bright side of trust and decency, the lard ass and his sons were out the door and on the way to their next 3,000 stops. This little drama played out three more times with three other bottom feeders. Then, a young kid from Ohio showed up, willing to abide by our rules. We sold him most of the inventory in exchange for wads of cash.

While this was playing out, I wheeled about town—most of which had not flooded, only our street and a bit along the river—to buy clothes and shoes to replace what I lost in the flood. A block from the Store, tucked right up against the railroad tracks was Old Bill's lawnmower repair shop. Old Bill, a good customer, had died a few weeks before the flood. The tiny shop had a two-room efficiency where he lived for years. I bought it for peanuts and slept there that night, right on Old Bill's dirty sheets and blankets.

Greta heard about it—I'd been staying with them—and had an old-fashioned German cleanliness fit. She came by the next morning and replaced every sheet, blanket, and towel with new ones. In my defense, I did empty the contents of his camper-size refrigerator. I'm not crazy. Though I did keep a tin of his coffee.

Every day felt different. Disasters destroy happy routines. But that's not what I mean. After my meltdown in front of the Store, three weeks ago now, the world felt different. I felt different. I wanted to get out of the goddamned creaky wheelchair and start walking again. I wanted to kick some fanny—anyone's fanny.

I wheeled over to the bank to see Bedford.

"I'm taking over for Robin, representing the company building the new hardware store."

"Jeez, Lord . . ."

"Lloyd."

"Lloyd. Really sorry to hear what happened. Do you have a signed POA statement?"

"I did. It got shanghaied in the post-flood turmoil."

"Never heard of a piece of paper being shanghaied."

"Tough world out there, Bed. Let me know when papers need to be signed. I'm in Old Bill's place, around the corner. I'll get you a phone."

Over the next few months, I made enough creative changes to Nine Mile's proposed plan for their hardware store to hold up their zoning approval for a year and a half. It didn't prove anything, and it didn't accomplish anything. It just felt good.

I drove out to the hospital and volunteered to talk to their wheelchair-bound patients. They'd been after me to do this for some time. Productive people in wheelchairs were still a rare sight in those years. They assumed that whatever I had to say would encourage paraplegics to get off their ass, so to speak.

These were not formal lectures. A group of eight or nine of us would make a circle in the lobby, or outside on the lawn, in summer. I would talk about my experiences for a bit, and this would precipitate a rolling conversation.

I did give a more formal talk to a class at the high school, and a series of three short presentations to a sociology class at Bucknell. Once I started talking, I couldn't stop. I even started a recurring column in our town newspaper, titled "My Chair Has Wheels." I wrote about everything from bathroom adventures to learning to drive with just hands. You could sense that interest in "the handicapped" was beginning to grow.

Life just happened. For the first time since my heady days at Albion, I began to exert myself. It seemed as if I had been dormant for almost thirty years. The flood washed away something. I didn't know what, but it felt good.

At one of my circle talks at the hospital, a kid in his late twenties, a veteran, told me he had been in his wheelchair for almost eight years. I asked him about his condition. Was there something wrong with him other than his spinal cord injury?

"Nope. I'm good."

"So, what have you been doing all these years?"

"Nothing. The VA takes care of me. They pay for everything."

"No job. What do you do all day?"

"Watch TV, sleep."

"For eight years?"

"Yep."

Without thinking about it, I wheeled over close to him, grabbed the seat of his wheelchair between his legs and flipped him over backward. He struck his head on the tile floor and flopped out of his chair.

"Next time I come out here, I better hear about you finding a job. Or, I'm going to lose my goddamn temper with you."

I left him there on the floor, scared half out of his mind—making little screeching sounds. A few months later, he was working as a patient processing specialist at the hospital, a paid position. I wasn't invited back, but it bothered me not.

Curiously, Bayer seemed more alive and in a better frame than I was. Once we sold off the damaged inventory and started to clean out the place, his mood changed. I think he felt liberated from twenty years of sailing a very slow ship. It caused me to reflect. His equanimity, his predictably calm approach to crisis large and small, was so appealing—probably why I tagged along with him all these years.

For me, the difference in our reaction to the life-changing flood captured *and* characterized a notion that had been in the back of my head since I was a kid. It starts with a question: Why are some people smarter, or perceived to be smarter, than others? This is not a simple notion. I began to think it had much to do with your outlook, your sense of optimism. While I perpetually tripped over a variety of problems, my outlook on life could be boiled down to "What now?"

Every new day brought a new problem. My mind was always keen to escape the new problem, duck away from the here and now. I read a lot/ I watched TV a lot. I stared out the window a lot.

Bayer's approach to life and problems was more "What have we here?" This more objective, call it more optimistic, approach to life allowed him to face *and* solve more of the problems encountered every day. While I tended to stew about things, he tended to act. He was always measuring, building, re-modeling.

"I have an idea," he said.

It was late October, four months since the flood. We had, with volunteer and hired help, gutted the Store. It looked like a big retail space, ready for a new business.

"Let's open a printing business. We'll work from Old Bill's shop. We'll do custom stationery, invitations, business cards."

"Do you know anything about printing?"

"My hobby as a kid."

A few weeks later, he sold the remnant of the Store to three guys who planned to open a café bar with space for special events—wedding receptions and the like. They seemed comfortable with the government weather experts' assessment that the big flood had been a hundred-year event. How does anyone know? But they read it somewhere and bought in. Bayer sold it for just enough to cover his costs, and a little extra. Of course, his plan for a comfortable retirement from the sale of a successful business was washed away with the flood waters.

A year later, the new Sun Graphics Printing Company was doing a humming business in the grim, cement-block room where Old Bill once repaired lawnmowers. We had two half-ton Chandler and Price letter presses, meticulously cranking out finely crafted wedding invitations, personal and business stationery, and custom business cards. We were actually making money. Not buckets, but enough to make life whole. And we were having fun—in a way.

I was flitting about the county in my own used truck, delivering printing jobs, procuring orders, and taking a renewed interest in people and their problems. I couldn't stop talking. I don't know why, and I didn't much care. Back at the shop, Bayer kidded me about this new turn.

"Maybe you should have gone into marketing or entertainment. Lewisburg seems a little small for you these days."

"Maybe I will. I think radio. Listeners won't see the wheelchair."

"You'll be a star in no time."

We were up to our elbows in ink stains, cranking both presses as fast as we could to complete an order of flyers, invitations, and mementos for Bucknell's annual homecoming festivities. The shop was a mess. Rejected proofs littered the floor. Open cans of ink sat on stools and on the counter. Bits of ink-stained rags were everywhere.

Old Bill hadn't wasted money on windows. We had extension cords and utility lights running up and down the cement block walls. A lot of press proofs were wedged behind these cords. We were a sorry sight, but we were cranking it out.

The front door opened and two tall BU students in formal dinner jackets and black tie entered. Poised, and unnaturally polished for men of such a young age, they even spoke in the slow cadence used by older men in positions of authority—judges and generals.

"We're here to pick up Days One and Two of the Homecoming materials."

As they paid, they talked about all the activities they were coordinating for the weekend.

Bayer said, "How did they pick you guys to do all the work?"

"When it's something important, they always come to us," said the slightly taller one. "We're TKEs."

Bayer looked at me with a wry smile. I'm not sure exactly what he meant. But I held my tongue. The young men left with the printing. We didn't talk for a couple minutes. Both presses had stopped, and the shop felt quieter and grimmer than usual.

That night, as I ate some soup and oyster crackers and waited for the midnight train to pass, I couldn't shake the image of those TKE brothers. Where would Bayer and I be today if I hadn't kicked him that night, if there had been no Depression, if Hirohito and Hitler had never been born—if Nine Mile had been a legit company? I could not imagine how we must have looked to those TKEs.

Someone knocked loudly on my door. My heart jumped. No one had yet knocked at my door, day or night. Then a woman's voice.

"Open up, Zadoc."

It's not as though I had a stable full of women, but I couldn't place the voice. I fumbled and stumbled to the door. A good-looking woman of medium height stood there, smiling. She had curly hair with traces of gray. She kept smiling, quietly laughing. I still had no . . . then I saw the white blouse and jean skirt.

"Skyler?"

She's laughing softly.

"Skyler!"

Now, she's laughing out loud.

"Sky-ler?"

Now, we're both laughing.

Chapter Thirty-Eight

You're killing me.

I can't help it. I like to reflect, sum things up, make sense of it all.

Would have been better if you had made sense while you were doing the things you're now trying to make sense of.

Don't be quaint.

***

I never did make sense of it all. Why did I foresee things? Why did I attach myself to Bayer and why did I end up living in Old Bill's railroad shack, working as a printer's assistant? And, why was I happy?

Nine Mile remained a mystery. Sometimes, I wondered if it was real or not—or just that liquid dollop of evil that sloshes about in everyone living outside the garden. And what the hell happened to my original plan, to steal cars and write comedies?

Even as I became more and more awake, bounced around town more, wrote more and more columns for the paper, met more people—even had lunch with the governor—the "what's it all about?" thing never let go of me.

So here I was, reclaiming my rightful role as Master of the Universe while not quite sure what I was Master of, and how I landed on this Universe. Of my original plan, I made what I thought was decent progress stealing cars—until I got behind the wheel of Bayer's enormous Packard De Luxe. And, I did write a couple comedies. They were good.

The first one, *Dog Germs*, was about this famous glass blower (I correctly apprehended that few comedies had been written about glass blowers) who has fallen into a creative slump. So, the artist decides to start wearing dresses rather than his usual canvas pants and wool shirts. He doesn't try to act any differently. He's not a cross-dresser; he still has the boxer shorts and steel-toed boots. But he refuses to explain to his wife, his apprentice, and his employees *why* he's wearing a dress. Everyone around him eventually over-reacts in some way, as each person trips over his or hers (or its) own footfalls. The chaos—and the human revelations—get the left and right side of our man's brain working together again, and creativity—and excellence in glass blowing—return as never before. And all is well—except for the wife, apprentice, and employees.

My second comedy was a riot. *Hamilton Dies, Hamilton Lives* is about this guy named Hamilton, who dies alone in a car accident on page one (which is a lonely place to die). Young Hamilton, whose only crime in life was that he was somewhat of a jerk in his relations with girl-friends, spends a quiet afternoon in Purgatory. There, he pleads with the staff, who, quite fortunately, are about his age, to give him a second chance at life. They finally agree, but with one condition: he must seek out his three ex-girlfriends and get at least one of them to accept his sincere apology. And so, Hamilton charges off to regain his footing on Earth, and soon runs into a problem he did not anticipate. Turns out, as much of a jerk as he was, he was far less a jerk than most guys. When he tries to apologize, he is met with, "Oh, stop it Hammy, you're making me like you all over again." The poor lad is reduced to desperation and tears, trying to save his second life.

So, stealing cars and writing comedies were not idle talk. I did them. And still, here I was, a printer's assistant, living in a clapboard railroad shack. And I was happy. And Skyler was standing in my door.

As I said, I never did figure it all out. But Skyler and I picked up our relationship—as girls like to say—from where we had left off. It blossomed into something much bigger and better than before. We never talked about her mother or Nine Mile—and we "got started" that very night, in earnest, even before the midnight train rattled past.

I just don't want to talk about it.

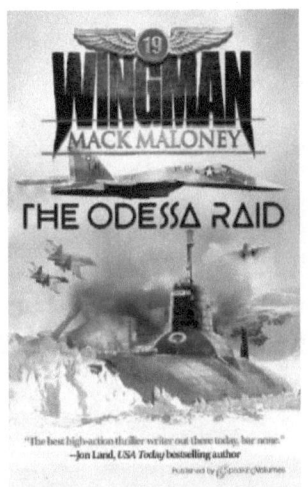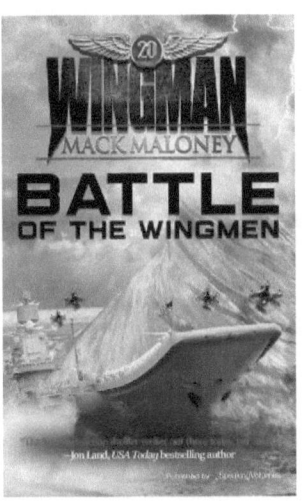

On Sale Now!

IAN SLATER

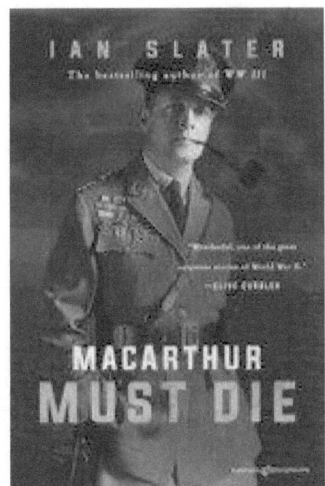

**For more information
visit:** www.SpeakingVolumes.us

On Sale Now!

CHARLES RYAN